D0052538

ADVENTURE TIME

WHICH WAY, DUDE?

#3

Lumpy Space Princess
Saves the World

WHICH WAY, DUDE?

#3

Lumpy Space Princess Saves the World

by Tracey West
illustrated by Ian McGinty

PSS!
PRICE STERN SLOAN
An Imprint of Penguin Group (USA) LLC

PRICE STERN SLOAN
Published by the Penguin Group
Penguin Group (USA) LLC, 375 Hudson Street, New York, New York 10014, USA

USA | Canada | UK | Ireland | Australia | New Zealand | India | South Africa | China

penguin.com
A Penguin Random House Company

If you purchased this book without a cover, you should be aware that this book is stolen property. It was reported as "unsold and destroyed" to the publisher, and neither the author nor the publisher has received any payment for this "stripped book."

Penguin supports copyright. Copyright fuels creativity, encourages diverse voices, promotes free speech, and creates a vibrant culture. Thank you for buying an authorized edition of this book and for complying with copyright laws by not reproducing, scanning, or distributing any part of it in any form without permission. You are supporting writers and allowing Penguin to continue to publish books for every reader.

The publisher does not have any control over and does not assume any responsibility for author or third-party websites or their content.

ADVENTURE TIME, CARTOON NETWORK, the logos, and all related characters and elements are trademarks of and © Cartoon Network. (s15)

Published in 2015 by Price Stern Sloan, a division of Penguin Young Readers Group, 345 Hudson Street, New York, New York 10014. *PSS!* is a registered trademark of Penguin Group (USA) LLC. Printed in the USA.

ISBN 978-0-8431-8078-7   10 9 8 7 6 5 4 3 2 1

OH MY GLOB, IT'S A DRAMA BOMB!

Help!

It's me, Lumpy Space Princess, and there's totally crazy stuff happening in Lumpy Space! Finn and Jake and Princess Bubblegum are all trying to help me, but, like, it's up to *you* to decide what happens.

This book is not like other lame books . . . so lumping pay attention, all right? Like, when you get to the end of each chapter, you'll have a choice to make—and sometimes you'll have to solve puzzles to help figure out what to do. So, like, don't mess it all up!

Along the way, you can earn **ADVENTURE MINUTES.** The more Adventure Minutes you earn, the more totally awesome your journey is. Whenever you earn Adventure Minutes, flip to page **121** so you can keep track of them. When you come to an ending, total up all your Adventure Minutes to figure out your total **ADVENTURE TIME!**

Good luck!

And don't be a chump . . . the future of Lumpy Space is in *your hands!*

1

BEGINNINGS
AND STUFF

"My parents are so lumping unfair!" Lumpy Space Princess grumbles as she floats across Ooo.

The Land of Ooo is loaded with princesses, but LSP is the only lumpy one. She looks like a purple cloud with bumps and arms, and she's got a yellow star in the middle of her forehead.

She's not nerdy like Princess Bubblegum, or hotheaded like the Flame Princess, or shy like the Turtle Princess. She's spoiled and her voice is totally annoying, but she's still friends with lots of people. She used to live in Lumpy Space, but after a major fight with her parents, she moved into a hotel room in Ooo.

As LSP passes the Candy Kingdom, she sees Princess Bubblegum. PB is yelling at a bunch of dopey Banana Guards. She stops when she sees her friend.

"Hey, LSP!" Princess Bubblegum calls out with a wave. "How's it going?"

"Lumping terrible, that's how!" she yells back, and then keeps going. She's too upset to talk to PB right now. She needs help from two heroes: Finn and Jake.

When she gets to their tree house, she finds them both outside. Jake is playing his violin under the shade of the tree, because he's cool like that. Finn is jumping around and waving a sword carved out of wood like he's pretend-fighting or something.

LSP floats right up to them.

"Finn! Jake! I'm so glad you're here. I need your help!" she cries.

Finn jumps in front of her. "What's up, LSP? You got an adventure for us?"

"I need you to come to Lumpy Space with me," she says. "It's an emergency!"

Jake is still playing his violin. Finn looks at him.

"Come on, dude. Let's go!"

Jake stops playing and sighs. "This better be good," he says. He knows that LSP can be totally full of drama—and not the exciting, monster-punching kind. Mostly just the whiny kind.

The three of them head toward the portal that will take them to Lumpy Space. It's the only way to get there, since nobody in Ooo has invented a working rocket ship yet.

"So, LSP, what's the emergency?" Finn asks, waving his sword in anticipation.

"It's my parents," she replies. "They're totally being lame! They won't let me borrow the car, and I need it because Melissa's car is being totally lame and broken, and we need to go to a party!"

Jake stops. "Okay. I'm out," he says, turning around.

"Jake, wait!" Finn says. "Come on, today has been totally boring. Going to Lumpy Space is better than just hanging around, right?"

"No," Jake says, still walking.

"Oh, come on, guys, I need you for moral support!" LSP pleads, her eyes tearing up. "My parents are being totally unfair."

"LSP, I thought you were, like, all independent and junk now," Finn points out.

"Mostly, but I don't have a car," LSP says. "And Melissa is my best friend. If I don't have a car, we can't hang out. It's lumping unfair!"

Finn and LSP stop in front of a weird-looking green frog sitting on a mushroom. Finn yells out to Jake.

"Hey, Jake, I'll bet you there's an adventure on the other side!"

Jake turns around. "Whatcha betting?"

Finn thinks. "Um . . . I'll make sandwiches for, like, a week."

"A month," Jake says.

"Fine," Finn agrees. Then he realizes something. "Hey, what do I get if I'm right?"

"You get an adventure, dude," Jake says.

The frog eyes them. "Password," he croaks.

"Whatevers 2009," LSP responds. "And don't give me a hard time about these nonlumpers. You've let them through before."

The frog opens his mouth wide and then, like, swallows all three of them! It's impossible, but possible because it's really happening.

They're, like, spinning and spiraling, and then they get dumped out onto a land lump. Lumpy Space is basically full of all these land lumps that look like giant clouds. Lumpy Space People live on them and get from one land lump to another by driving these space cars, only they look just like regular cars.

The land lump they land on is home of the king and queen

of Lumpy Space—LSP's parents. Because they're married, their bodies are joined together into one big lump with two heads. And now they're screaming both heads off.

"Heeeeeeeeeeelp!"

Lumpy Space is in total chaos. There's a big black hole in the starry sky that's just sucking everything up. Lumpy Space People are spiraling through space into the hole.

"Rats! No sandwiches," Jake says. He wraps his rubbery legs around a lump sticking out of the ground, and then wraps his body around Finn and LSP to keep them from getting sucked in.

"Mom! Dad!" LSP cries. She watches in horror as her parents get sucked into the black hole thingy. Because even though she's mad at them, they're still her parents and she loves them.

She looks at Finn and Jake. "This is all your fault!"

So what will they all do now?

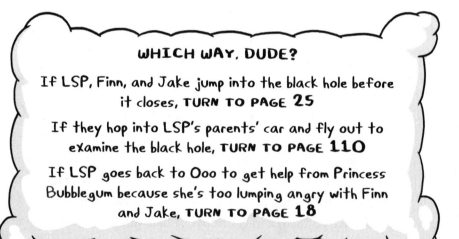

WHICH WAY, DUDE?

If LSP, Finn, and Jake jump into the black hole before it closes, **TURN TO PAGE 25**

If they hop into LSP's parents' car and fly out to examine the black hole, **TURN TO PAGE 110**

If LSP goes back to Ooo to get help from Princess Bubblegum because she's too lumping angry with Finn and Jake, **TURN TO PAGE 18**

THE REAL BRAD?

LSP goes to the cell on the right.

"Nebula Aluben!" she says, repeating the witch's spell, and the bars slide open. Brad steps out.

"Brad? Is it really you?" LSP asks.

"Yes," Brad answers.

LSP crushes him in a hug. "Oh, Brad, we've got to get out of this horrible place!"

"Sure," Brad says. He doesn't have much of a personality, but there must be something special about him, right? Or else why would LSP be so into him?

"So, I'm thinking," Finn interrupts, "that maybe we should find that Space Witch and make her call off that monster and magic everybody he ate out of his belly, or whatever. 'Cause even if we get out of here, we've still got that monster to fight."

"I think we have a better chance with the monster than with the witch," Jake says.

"Maybe," Finn says. "But anyway, we can't just stand around here, right?"

"Brad, do you know the way out?" LSP asks.

Brad shrugs. "No. This place is like a maze."

They make their way through the twisty, turny prison. The whole time, LSP can't stop talking to Brad.

"It's, like, totally amazing that we found each other in this place," she's saying. "I mean, like, it's destiny, right? I know you're with Melissa, but you can't ignore destiny. Nobody can ignore destiny. That would be lame."

"Mmm-hmm," Brad says.

"And if Melissa has a problem, I'll just be like, you can't ignore destiny, Melissa. You just can't."

"Yeah," Brad says.

Jake's head is starting to hurt. LSP's voice is more annoying than being attacked by a swarm of swamp beetles.

"Does this place ever end?" he mumbles.

They turn a corner and come to a door marked DO NOT ENTER.

"It must be the witch's secret lair," Finn says. "Let's check it out!"

He opens the door and they go in. The door slams behind them. The room is dark.

"Here's a light switch," Jake says, and flicks it on.

Aaaaaaah! The room is totally filled with giant space spiders with glowing eyes! Jake runs to the door, but he can't get it open.

Finn starts slashing at the spiders with his sword.

Whoosh! His sword goes right through one, and it flickers.

"Hey! They're just, like, holograms or something!" Finn cries.

He slashes at another spider.

Hiss! This one is real. It shoots yellow liquid from its fangs, and Finn dodges it.

"What the lump is going on?" LSP yells.

"Some are real and some are fake," Finn says. "We've got to fight the real ones."

★ ★ You earn 36 ADVENTURE MINUTES. ★ ★

HELP THE GANG PICK OUT THE FAKE SPIDERS

The fake spiders have white eyes. The real spiders have black eyes. Circle all the real spiders you see. How many are there?

If you think there are more than 12 real spiders,
TURN TO PAGE 31

If you think there are fewer than 12 real spiders,
TURN TO PAGE 70

M
IS FOR MAJA

Lumpy Space Princess and Princess Bubblegum hurry through the Flower Path as the Fruit Witches chase them. Suddenly they see a light at the end of the tunnel. They pass through it . . .

. . . and find themselves in a dark, dusty, spiderwebby old house.

"Maja the Sky Witch," PB says in a whisper. She has been here before.

"This is super creepy," LSP says.

"Maja's a pretty serious witch," Princess Bubblegum says. "She'd make a great scientist if she wasn't so obsessed with all this dark, spooky stuff."

Suddenly, they hear a voice behind them.

"What's wrong with dark, spooky stuff?"

It's Maja! Her skin is the color of pea soup, and she wears her dark hair in a bun on top of her head. She's got legs, but her long cloak covers them, and she floats like LSP.

"Witch!" LSP yells, and she freaks out. She rushes through the nearest door.

PB follows her. "LSP, wait!"

LSP has flown into Maja's cauldron room. There's a big cauldron bubbling in the middle, and lots of shelves with books and potions and junk. LSP is banging into stuff like a pinball in a machine. She knocks over a bunch of stuff.

Maja follows them in. "You bubbleheaded dolts! I was going to invite you for a cup of tea. But you've ticked me off. Clean this up exactly the way you found it, or I'll turn you both into toads!"

★ ★ You earn 73 ADVENTURE MINUTES. ★ ★

HELP LSP AND PB FIX THE CAULDRON ROOM

The first picture shows the cauldron room before LSP messed it up. The second picture shows what it looked like after. Circle all the things PB messed up.

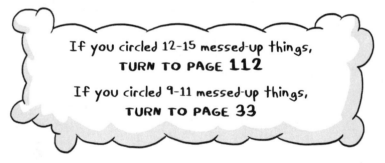

If you circled 12-15 messed-up things,
TURN TO PAGE 112

If you circled 9-11 messed-up things,
TURN TO PAGE 33

WHEN RIGHT
IS WRONG

"Let's go through this tunnel," LSP says, floating through the tunnel on the right. Finn and Jake follow her as the monster snaps its huge jaws behind them.

The tunnel leads to a metal door. They open it and step into a metal room. The door slams behind them.

"Where are we?" LSP asks.

Jake turns around and points to a sign on the wall:

WELCOME TO THE UNBEARABLE CHAMBER OF ENDLESS BOREDOM.

"That doesn't sound good," says Finn.

He and Jake and LSP all try to open the door, but they can't. Jake can't even make himself super tiny and crawl under it.

"It must be magically sealed," Jake guesses. "Looks like we're stuck here."

"Finn and Jake, this is all your fault!" wails LSP.

THE END

A FRUITFUL
FINISH

LSP and PB make their way through the Flower Path. They end up at a dead end: a table piled high with fruit.

"Eat!" yells the blond witch, shoving an apple into LSP's mouth.

"Eat!" commands the brunette witch, feeding PB a peach.

The princesses can't fight the powerful magic of the witches.

Poof! LSP turns into a giant apple.

Poof! PB turns into a giant peach.

The Fruit Witches descend on them. The white teeth of their hair-creatures are snapping with anticipation.

"I'm guessing we're about to be eaten!" says PB.

"Oh my glob!" wails LSP. "We're doomed!"

THE END

THE GuARDIAN
OF THE GUTS

Kablam! Kablam! Kablam! Jake squirts every cell with the canned cheese. They explode, leaving orange and green gunk everywhere. But that's okay, because at least the gang can escape.

"Help us! Help us!"

The cries of the Lumpy Space People are even louder now.

"It's coming from this tube," LSP says, pointing. "Mom and Dad, don't worry! I'm coming!"

She floats through the tube, and Finn and Jake jump in after her. They don't get far, because the tube kind of curves and they get stuck. Then they hear a voice.

"Hey! Watch where you're going!"

They look and see a really, really old Candy Corn Dude hanging out in the tube. In the Candy Kingdom, Candy Corn Dudes have three faces: one white, one yellow, and one orange. But all you can see on this dude is the white face on the top, because he's got a long white beard that goes all the way down to his feet.

"*You* watch where *you're* going," LSP shoots back.

"I'm not the one moving around," Candy Corn Dude says. "I'm stuck. Can't you see?"

Suddenly it's obvious that the Candy Corn Dude is stuck in the tube. He's kind of dangling there.

"Dude, how long have you been stuck?" Finn asks.

The Candy Corn Dude strokes his beard. "Hmm. A long time now, I think. I was just a tiny sweet when I got sucked in here."

Finn reaches up. "We can free you!"

"No!" the old dude yells. "I like it just fine here."

"What are you talking about?" LSP asks. "It's super lame here."

"I am the Guardian of the Guts! It is my sacred duty to guard them," he replies. "Besides, all my friends are here."

There's clearly nobody else in the tube. But the Guardian of the Guts is waving and smiling at his imaginary friends.

"I think he's gone loopy after being stuck in here all these years," Jake whispers to Finn.

"Yeah, but we should rescue him anyway," Finn whispers back.

"No way. He looks too happy," Jake argues.

"Whatever!" LSP yells. "Old guy, have you seen my parents?" she asks the Candy Corn Dude.

"What do they look like?" the Guardian of the Guts asks.

"They're good-looking and lumpy, like me," LSP says. "They got sucked in here with a whole bunch of other Lumpy Space People a little while ago."

Candy Corn Dude nods. "I didn't see them, but I heard them. I know where they are."

"Then tell us how to find them!" LSP demands.

The weird old guy chuckles. "It's not that easy. Nobody gets past the Guardian of the Guts without answering a riddle."

"Seriously?" LSP asks. Then she sighs. "Whatever. What's the stupid riddle?"

The guardian's eyes gleam. "Okay, here's your riddle: 'I am in your guts. You'll find me coming and going. Without me, there would be no gravity.' What am I?"

★★ You earn 33 ADVENTURE MINUTES. ★★

SHADE IN ALL THE SHAPES WITH THREE SIDES TO FIND THE ANSWER TO THE RIDDLE.

If the answer to the riddle is the letter "G,"
TURN TO PAGE 72

If the answer to the riddle is the letter "C,"
TURN TO PAGE 45

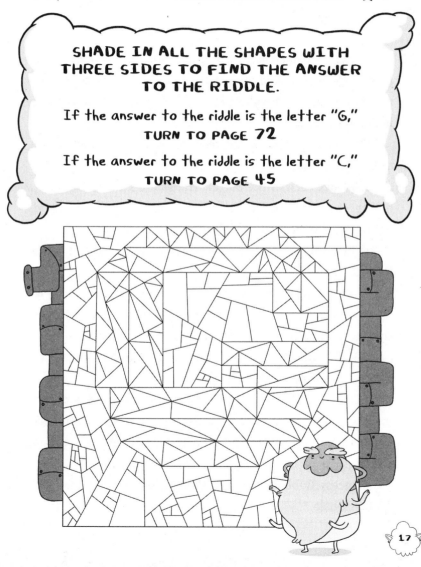

A TaLE OF
TWO PRINCESSES

LSP is super steamed at Finn and Jake. She blames them for her parents getting sucked up into the black hole even though it's not their fault. But they're the closest to her, and she wants to blame somebody.

"I'm getting Princess Bubblegum!" she yells. "She's smart, at least, and not lame like you two!"

LSP goes back to the portal. Things are swirly-whirly for a few seconds, and then she's back in Ooo, in the Cotton Candy Forest. She hurries to PB's palace as fast as she can.

When she gets there, the princess is still talking to her Banana Guards.

"Okay, now, what's our visitor policy again?" she's asking.

"No more hanging them upside down by their ankles unless they do something bad," the guards drone in one voice.

"Good!" says PB. Then she notices LSP. "LSP, what's wrong? You look more upset than before."

"It's terrible!" LSP wails. "I was in Lumpy Space with Finn and Jake, and then this black hole started sucking up everybody, and it took my parents! And Finn and Jake didn't do anything to stop it!"

Princess Bubblegum looks thoughtful. "Hmm," she says. "A black hole."

"We've got to get them out!" cries LSP.

"That may not be possible," says PB. "But I'm not entirely sure."

LSP gets all mad. "You know, I wasn't surprised when Finn and Jake let me down. But you're smarter! I really thought you could help me! But you're just lame."

Princess Bubblegum's eyes narrow. She may look all sweet, with her pink candy skin and her pink bubble gum hair, but she's a supercompetitive genius, too. Plus, she really wants to help her friend.

"There's a book on black holes in the Turtle Princess's library," she says. "Let's go get it."

TURN TO PAGE 48

FIVE REALLY SHORT GRAYBLES

The Pagelings whisk LSP and PB into a book called *Five Really Short Graybles*. Then they disappear. The two princesses are left facing a strange dude with a big, round, bald head and a short body with skinny arms and no legs.

"Ho ho, gleeble bayble grapes!" he greets them. "Bayble Cuber has five really short stories for you—each relating to one special theme. See if you Graybles can figure it out by the end of the book, okay?"

"What the lump are you saying?" LSP asks.

Princess Bubblegum grabs her by the hand. "We have to read five stories and figure out what they have in common. Let's hurry up and get this over with!"

"See you on the glimping flip side!" Cuber says with a wave.

"This is lame!" LSP complains. "Those annoying paper guys just dumped us here."

"It shouldn't take us too long," PB says. "Look, there's Abracadaniel! The stories must be starting."

Abracadaniel is a skinny wizard who's all about butterflies and rainbows and stuff. Right now he's packing junk into a box.

"What are you doing, Abracadaniel?" PB asks.

"A big bad wolf is coming!" Abracadaniel replies. "I'm packing up all my things so he doesn't steal them."

LSP looks in the box. She sees apples, an abacus, a stuffed aardvark, and an accordion.

"This stuff is lame," LSP says.

"It's not lame. It's magic!" Abracadaniel says. He picks up the accordion and starts to play. As the honking music pours out of it, a rainbow appears above his head. "See?"

Then Abracadaniel stops playing and throws the accordion into the box. "Gotta run! The wolf is coming."

Abracadaniel runs off. The princesses keep walking, and soon they see their friend Engagement Ring Princess. She's got blue skin and pink hair, and she always wears a fancy dress. Her crown isn't a regular crown—it's an engagement ring. Right now she's sitting under a tree, reading.

"What are you doing, Engagement Ring Princess?" PB asks.

"Just reading the latest issue of *Elegant Weddings*. There's a beautiful eggshell wedding gown in here," the princess replies. She sighs. "I would love to get married to a handsome prince someday."

Then a tiny blue elephant waddles up.

"Maybe this is a handsome prince in disguise!" Engagement Ring Princess says. She picks up the elephant and kisses it. Nothing happens. "Oh well."

"Boring!" complains LSP.

TURN TO PAGE 91

21

LUMPY
SPACE MONSTER

"What?" Brad asks.

LSP drags him to her parents' car and pulls him inside. Then she speeds away.

"LSP, we can't fight this monster by ourselves," says Brad.

"I know. But Dad has a saying. If you can't beat them, join them," says LSP.

"How is that going to lumping help?" Brad asks.

LSP doesn't answer him. She's pretty peeved at Brad. But she needs his help for her plan.

The monster is waving the tentacle things that are all over its body. They're super creepy, and LSP has to dodge them so they don't hit the car. She steers toward the monster's back and lands on its black, blobby flesh.

She leans out of the car, opens her mouth, and bites the monster!

"What are you doing?" Brad asks.

"Stop talking and start biting," LSP demands. "Like, now!"

Brad knows he can't argue with LSP. He starts biting the monster. LSP keeps biting, too. Soon, lumps start popping up all over the monster's body.

Why? Because Lumpy Space People are kind of like werewolves. If they bite you, you get all lumpy like them. It happened to Finn and Jake once, but they used an antidote to get better.

"Oh my glob, what are all these Lumpy Space People doing in my gut?" Carl asks in his deep, thunderous space monster voice. "This is so lumping weird. Gross!"

Then Carl starts coughing. He coughs up all the Lumpy Space People! They fall onto the land lumps below.

"Get the lump out of me!" Carl yells. "I'm outta here. I've got to show all the other monsters my awesome new lumps."

Carl floats away, and LSP drives back to the land lumps with Brad. She's got a funny taste in her mouth, but otherwise she feels pretty great.

As soon as the car lands, Melissa runs up to it. She's all lumpy and pink, and looks very relieved.

"Oh, Brad! You're all right!" she says in her high voice, and gives him a kiss on the cheek.

LSP feels crummy. But then Finn and Jake run up to the car, along with her parents and a bunch of Lumpy Space People.

"Nice job, LSP," Jake says.

"LSP is a hero!" Finn yells.

Everyone claps and cheers.

"Oh, come on, guys, it was nothing," LSP says modestly, but inside she's feeling super awesome. Maybe she doesn't have Brad, but that's okay. She feels like a hero!

★ ★ You earn 88 ADVENTURE MINUTES. ★ ★

THE END

SWARMED!

"This is lame! I am not going to keep talking!" LSP says, and then she clams up.

"Aw, come on, LSP!" Jake pleads, but she just won't do it.

Without LSP's voice to repel the bacteria, they are in trouble. The neon-blue creatures swarm them, jabbing at LSP, Finn, and Jake with their spikes. LSP's lumps start to feel weird. They are getting spiky, not lumpy. She looks down at herself. She's turning blue.

Jake and Finn are turning blue, too!

"I think we're transforming into these gnarly dudes," says Jake.

"Gross! Okay! I'll keep talking!" LSP promises . . . but it's too late!

THE END

NOT A REGULAR
BLACK HOLE

The black hole is starting to get smaller and less sucky.

"We've got to rescue my parents!" LSP yells.

"Right," agrees Jake, and he unwraps his body from the lump anchoring them and then *whoosh!* The black hole sucks all three of them up into the air.

"We're coming to save you!" Finn yells as they're pulled up across the blackness of space.

"My lumps!" LSP cries.

They don't know what is waiting for them inside the black hole. Will they just spiral on and on for eternity? Is there, like, a whole new world on the other side?

Suddenly, they enter the hole.

Squish!

That's the sound they make when they're inside. They bounce against some smooshy, fleshy stuff.

"Gross!" says Finn. "What is all this squishy junk?"

"It's pretty smelly in here," Jake adds.

"Who cares? Where are my parents?" LSP asks.

Now that nobody is talking, they can hear faint cries for help in the distance.

"We've got to go deeper inside," Finn says.

Finn and Jake realize they can stand on the fleshy stuff.

It's really dark, but their eyes start to get used to things.

"This is freaky, dude," Jake says. "I kinda think we're inside something alive."

"You mean, like, some giant monster that ate us?" Finn asks. "Cool! See, I knew we would find an adventure here!"

They squish along for a while, and then Finn steps into nothingness.

"Whoooooaaaaa!" he yells as he starts to fall.

Jake reaches out with his rubbery arm. He grabs Finn and pulls him back up.

"Thanks, dude," Finn says.

LSP looks down the hole Finn just fell into. She can see all these crazy tubes.

"Monster guts!" says Jake.

The sound of the yelling Lumpy Space People is a little louder now. But it's hard to tell which tube they should go down.

★ ★ You earn 4 ADVENTURE MINUTES. ★ ★

HELP LSP, FINN, AND JAKE GET TO LSP'S PARENTS

On the next page, navigate the maze to find where the Lumpy Space People are inside this monster body. Will you find them—or find something much worse?

If you ended up at A, **TURN TO PAGE 96**

If you ended up at B, **TURN TO PAGE 109**

THE Ice QUEEN'S
WEDDING

"Where are we?" LSP asks.

"Let's see. We're in the overall section for A–M. But it looks like we're in the *I* aisle," Princess Bubblegum replies. "I'll look under *intergalactic*."

Even though she's anxious to save her parents, space stuff is boring to LSP. She starts browsing the titles.

"*Ibis in Love. Ice Cream Recipes. The Ice Queen's Wedding,*" LSP reads aloud. Then she stops. "*The Ice Queen's Wedding?* That is the lumping boring fan fiction that the Ice King writes! What the lump is this trash doing in the library?"

She knows about it because the Ice King loves to read his fan fiction out loud to his captured princesses. They're the only ones who will listen, because nobody else wants to hear about junk from the Ice King's imagination. The only thing is, the stories are actually kind of interesting.

In his fan fiction, Ice King turns all the boys into girls, and all the girls into boys. So Finn is a girl named Fionna. Jake is a cat named Cake. The Ice King is the Ice Queen. It's like that with everybody in Ooo.

LSP can't help herself. She picks up the book and opens it. She doesn't notice the magical, wizardy purple mist floating all around it.

28

Whoosh! She and PB get sucked right inside the book! Like, not physically slammed into the pages—they get turned into characters in the book. That's wizard magic for you.

"Oh my glob!" LSP cries. Because one second ago, they were in the library, and now they're in the Ice Kingdom. She hasn't figured out yet that they're in the book.

"Interesting," says PB. "Have we been transported to the Ice Kingdom?"

A Candy Kingdom citizen walks past, and PB stops him.

"Excuse me, but can you tell me where you're going?" PB asks.

"Sure, lady," says the piece of taffy. "It's the Ice Queen's wedding! Everyone's invited." And then the taffy hurries off.

Princess Bubblegum is a smart cookie. She knows the taffy didn't recognize her, because he called her "lady." And the Ice Queen isn't real—she's only in stories. Therefore . . .

"LSP, what book were you holding before we were transported?" PB asks.

"*The Ice Queen's Wedding,*" LSP says. "Why?"

"Because I think we were transported inside the book," PB says.

"What? How do we get out?" LSP asks.

"Well, I think we have to go through the story," says PB. "When we get to the end, we should be able to leave the book. Theoretically, anyway."

"So let's do it," LSP says. "Let's go to this lame wedding and then get out of here."

They walk up to the Ice Queen's castle, where penguins are letting everyone inside. Everybody is handing over tickets. The penguins take them and then tear them up.

"I have an idea," PB says. She swipes one of the torn-up tickets. "We'll piece this together and use it to get in."

★ ★ You earn 51 ADVENTURE MINUTES. ★ ★

ARRANGE THE LETTER PIECES TO PUT THE TICKET TOGETHER.

es AD WO TT MI TS GU

If you think the ticket is for TWO GUESTS, TURN TO PAGE 83

If you think the ticket is for TWO TWITS, TURN TO PAGE 88

YO,
SPACE WITCH!

Squish! Squash! Squoosh! Finn quickly takes out all the real space spiders. It's good that he knows which ones are fake so he doesn't waste time on them.

They leave the room through a door on the other side. *Bam!* They're in the Space Witch's headquarters or whatever. There's, like, a big computer-looking machine with lights in crazy colors. Cages hang from the ceiling with weird creatures in them. And there's the Space Witch, too. Her star-shaped eyes flash with anger when she sees them.

"You got out! No way!" she cries, and then she points her fingers at them.

"Duck!" Finn cries, but it's too late. Astrid yells out a spell as the lasers hit them.

"Parsec Cesrap!" she yells.

Finn, Jake, and Brad are totally frozen. They're like statues. But LSP is still floating around. For some reason, the witch doesn't freeze her.

"What did you do to them?" LSP wails.

"I don't need them," Astrid says, and her star eyes flash. "I need you."

"What are you talking about?" asks LSP.

"I'm working on a new spell, and I need some powerful

magic for it," she says. She nods at frozen Brad. "I see the way you look at that blue one. Why, I'm not sure. But you've got some strong feelings there. If you give up the part of your heart that loves him, I'll free your friends."

LSP is stunned. "What about my parents?" she asks.

"I'll get Carl to cough them up, along with all your lumpy friends," the witch says. "What do you say? Do we have a deal?"

WHAT SHOULD LSP DO?

In this puzzle, look for the space words on the list and circle them. You can find them up, down, across, backward, and diagonally. The remaining letters will spell out what LSP should do.

ASTEROID
COMET
GALAXY
METEOR
MOON
NOVA
PLANET
SPACE
STARS
SUN
ORBIT

```
M G I O R B I T
O E S U N V G E
O I T T T T A S
N S T E N A L P
N R O M O A A A
O A S O T R X C
V T R C I D Y E
A S T E R O I D
```

If LSP refuses to give up her love for Brad,
TURN TO PAGE 90

If LSP makes the sacrifice to save her people,
TURN TO PAGE 113

S IS FOR
SPACE WITCH

"Good job," Maja says when she returns to check the cauldron room. "I'm a witch of my word. Now get out of here before I change my mind."

"Thanks, Maja," PB says pleasantly as they leave the room. They head down the creaky stairs and out the front door. They open the door . . . but they're not outside.

They're in a big room with metal walls. The room is filled with strange creatures in cages. There's a portal in the wall, and outside, they can see the blackness of space, dotted with stars.

"Hmm," says PB. "This encyclopedia of witches is divided into witch types. Maybe this is some kind of Space Witch?"

"This is getting ridiculous," says LSP. "Are we ever going to get out of this book?"

But PB is fascinated with the creatures in the room.

"Amazing," she says, eyeing a tank with a rainbow-colored creature covered with tentacles.

"PB, let's get out of here!" LSP pleads.

Then PB notices a poster on the wall. It shows a giant, black blobby space monster with a huge mouth. It's labeled: CARL.

"Look, LSP!" she says. "This poster says that this Carl monster has an enormous mouth that sucks things up like a black hole. I bet that's what swallowed your parents!"

"Oh my glob!" LSP says. "We'll never save them now."

"Maybe we can," PB says. "There's a word here—a command. The witch uses it to control Carl. Maybe we can use it, too."

Then an alarm sounds.

"Intruders in the menagerie!" says a monotone voice.

"Quick! Hide!" PB hisses.

LSP quickly looks for a hiding place. But she's freaking out, and *bam*! She knocks over a tank. That knocks over another tank. And another tank. Now there are weird creatures splashing around in a puddle on the floor.

"Oh no!" she wails.

"Quick! Let's put them back before the witch gets here!" PB says.

They get all the creatures back just in time— except for one.

THE WITCH IS GETTING
CLOSER! ON THE NEXT PAGE
HELP LSP GET THE CREATURE
BACK IN THE CORRECT TANK.

If you think the creature goes in Tank A,
TURN TO PAGE 52

If you think the creature goes in Tank B,
TURN TO PAGE 80

WITcH
VS.
PRINcESS

LSP floats to the cell on the left.

"Nebula Aluben!" she yells, repeating the witch's spell. The bars slide open, and Brad steps out.

"Oh, Brad!" she cries, hugging him. But suddenly Brad doesn't feel lumpy anymore—he feels bony. LSP steps back. She's hugging the Space Witch!

"What a chump!" says Astrid. "Tricked you with a simple transformation spell. But I'm pretty ticked that you guys got out of your cell. So, I think I'll just destroy you."

She wiggles her magic fingers, and LSP slaps them away.

"You are making me super mad!" LSP yells. "Get Brad out of this prison! And get my parents out of that stupid monster."

Astrid cackles. "How are you going to make me do that?"

LSP's eyes narrow. "I challenge you to a duel."

"Well, sure, but that would be unfair, wouldn't it?" Astrid asks. "You don't have any magic."

"I don't need magic," LSP says. "I have my lumps!"

Finn gives Jake a worried look.

"Hey, LSP, are you sure about this?" Finn calls out.

"You bet!" LSP says. "Bring it on, witch!"

"Have it your way!" Astrid shoots back. Her starry eyes flash. "Saros Soras!"

She transforms into a wicked-looking giant blue snake with stars for eyes. Finn pulls his sword.

"I got this, Finn," LSP says. She concentrates really hard, and her lumps start to move and change. In a few seconds, she looks like a mongoose—a fierce mammal that kills snakes.

The giant witch-snake squeals and slithers away. LSP, Finn, and Jake chase her. She goes into a room that's like a big indoor garden, with trees and junk growing. They can't see her right away.

"Where did she go?" Jake wonders.

Then the floor begins to shake. A blue dragon with star-shaped eyes crashes through the trees. They can see a fireball burning in her throat.

"Watch out, LSP!"

LSP transforms into an elephant with a long trunk. She dips the trunk in a fountain of water under the trees.

The witch-dragon shoots out a ball of fire. Elephant-LSP shoots water at it. The fire goes out!

"I win!" LSP cries.

"This isn't over yet!" Astrid yells back. "Axis Sixa!"

Astrid turns into a big blue towel and starts to mop up the water. LSP morphs her lumps until she looks like an iron.

"I'll flatten you!" LSP says.

Astrid transforms again. This time, it blows LSP's mind.

Astrid is all lumpy. She's blue, not pink, but otherwise she looks like LSP's best friend, Melissa!

"Melissa? But how?" LSP asks.

"I can see into your mind," Astrid says. "Come on, try and hurt your best friend. I bet you can't."

★ ✖ **You earn 50 ADVENTURE MINUTES.** ★ ✖

HELP LSP DEFEAT ASTRID

What should LSP turn into next? Solve this double-scrambled puzzle to find out. Unscramble the names of these three *Adventure Time* characters. Write the names in the blanks. Then unscramble the circled letters to find out what LSP should turn into next. If you get it wrong, she'll lose the battle!

RATPY DOG

_ _ _ _ _ _ _ _

CLEAMNIRE

_ _ _ _ _ _ _ _ _

LILBY

_ _ _ _ _

LSP should turn into a

_ _ _ _ _ .

If LSP morphs into a beard, **TURN TO PAGE 111**

If LSP morphs into a bread, **TURN TO PAGE 54**

SMAsH!

"Leave it to me, LSP," Jake says. He doesn't need a space car to get up there—he just stretches his whole body. Up, up, and up he goes until he gets to the meteor.

The space rock is bigger than Jake. He pulls and pulls, but he can't get it out.

The monster starts to giggle. Jake is tickling him!

The monster is laughing hard now. Between the laughing and the pulling, the meteor pops out and floats away.

But the monster can't stop laughing. It's laughing so hard that it rolls over on one of the land lumps.

Smash! It crushes a bunch of houses.

"No way! Lame!" LSP cries.

The monster rolls over again, on another land lump.

Smash! More houses crushed.

Smash! The monster crushes stuff on a third land lump. Then it floats away. Jake unstretches.

"Well, at least the monster's gone," Jake says.

"Thanks for nothing, Jake!" LSP says angrily.

THE END

INTO
THE PIT!

"Muzela Alezum!" LSP cries.

They hope the door of the cell will open. Instead, the bottom of the cell drops out!

"*Aaaaaaaaaaaaaah!*" yell Finn, Jake, and LSP as they fall, and fall, and fall, and then . . .

Splash! They've landed in some gross, murky pit of water.

"Heeeeelp!" Finn yells, splashing and flailing around. He can't swim and has this deep, primal fear of water. Luckily, Jake knows all about it. He quickly pulls Finn up onto the rocky ledge that surrounds the pit.

LSP floats up to them. "What the lump happened?"

"I think you read the wrong spell, LSP," Finn says, shivering and shaking the water off him.

"Well, that's not *my* fault," she shoots back.

Jake sees something across the pool. There are two tunnels carved into the rocky wall.

"Looks like a way out," Jake says.

"No way am I swimming over there!" Finn protests.

Jake stretches his body across the pool, making a bridge. "You don't have to swim. Come on!"

Finn starts to walk across, and LSP floats next to him. Then the water begins to churn.

"Uh-oh," says Finn. "What's that?"

Two huge eyes slowly rise out of the water. It's a giant beast! Is it friendly?

Nobody wants to find out.

"Hurry!" yells Jake.

Finn and LSP cross the Jake-bridge as the monster rears up. It's got a mouth full of long teeth as sharp as knives.

Snap! It almost bites Jake in half!

Jake quickly retracts his body. Finn slips into the water, but he grips the rocky ledge just in time. He pulls himself up.

Snap! The monster tries to bite Finn's legs!

Finn jumps up onto the ledge. There are two tunnels in front of him.

"Which tunnel should we go through?" LSP asks.

★ ✱ **You earn 10 ADVENTURE MINUTES.** ★ ✱

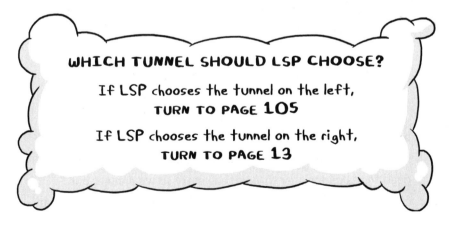

WHICH TUNNEL SHOULD LSP CHOOSE?

If LSP chooses the tunnel on the left,
TURN TO PAGE 105

If LSP chooses the tunnel on the right,
TURN TO PAGE 13

THE WITCHES
OF OOO

"Where are we?" LSP asks.

"Let's see. We're in the overall section for N–Z. But it looks like we're in the *W* aisle," Princess Bubblegum replies. "We should find the *S* aisle and see if there are any books on space."

"Whatever," says LSP. She floats after PB, and as she does, a book falls off the shelf.

"*Witches of Ooo*," LSP reads out loud. "Who needs that? There should be a book on princesses!"

As she talks, the book opens up. The magic mist from the wizard's ball snakes out and touches LSP and PB. Then *whoosh*! Everything changes.

They're not in the library anymore. Instead, they're in a big white space with words floating in the air: THE WITCHES OF OOO.

"What the lump?" LSP asks.

PB looks thoughtful. "It's just a theory, but I think we've been sucked inside the book, thanks to the wizard's gadget. And since books progress in a linear sequence, I'm guessing we just need to make our way through the story so we can get out."

"What kind of story is this?" LSP wonders, looking up at the title.

"It's an encyclopedia, I think," PB responds. "Come on, let's walk and see what we find."

PB and LSP make their way across the white plains. Then the scene changes. They're in a peaceful tunnel the color of a young peach. White blossoms and flower petals are gently falling down. Calm music is playing in the background.

"Ooh, pretty," LSP says.

"And dangerous," says Princess Bubblegum. "This is the Flower Path of the Fruit Witches."

"Fruit Witches?" asks LSP. "They don't sound dangerous."

"But they are," says PB. "Trust me."

Suddenly, two Fruit Witches appear. Their skin is pale green, and their green eyes are like the eyes of snakes. One has long, flowing blond hair, and the other has short, thick brown hair. They're spooky and pretty at the same time.

"Princesses!" says one witch.

"Please, stay and eat with us!" the other one says.

"LSP, move it!" PB yells, and she charges past the two witches. LSP floats behind her as fast as she can.

"Why are we leaving?" LSP asks.

"Look behind you!" PB yells.

LSP obeys. The two witches are flying after them. Now LSP can see that a wicked-looking black creature is sticking out of the hair of each witch. Each creature has eyes as red as blood, and sharp white teeth.

"Gross!" LSP wails, and hurries after PB.

★ ✹ You earn 47 ADVENTURE MINUTES. ★ ✹

CLIK
THE ROBOT

"You're so wrong!" says the Guardian of the Guts.

"What? Does that mean you're not going to tell us how to find my parents?" LSP asks angrily.

"Right," says the guardian.

LSP floats right up into his face. "Listen to me, you rotten old guy. You tell me where to find my parents. RIGHT. NOW!"

"Whoa, she's pretty steamed," Jake whispers to Finn.

The old Candy Corn Dude shrugs. "Okay," he says, pointing. "Head down that tube right there."

Finn is suspicious. "Uh, LSP, are you sure we should trust this guy? I mean—"

But LSP has already floated down the tube that the Guardian of the Guts pointed to.

"Might as well," Jake says, and he and Finn jump in after her.

They slide down the twisty, turny tube like it's a waterslide. Then . . . *bump!* They land on something squishy. They're in another part of the monster's body. This one is filled with bubbling puddles of green ooze. LSP is there, and also . . . a robot?

"What are you doing in here, dude?" Finn asks.

The robot doesn't look like any robot they've ever seen. It's not tiny and cute, like Finn and Jake's friend BMO. It's not made of candy machine parts, like Princess Bubblegum would use. This guy has two eyes that look like soda cans with lightbulbs inside them. Its body is a rectangle made of metal. It has metal arms with metal hands on the end, and metal legs and feet.

"My name is Clik. I was swallowed by the monster," the robot explains. "And the Guardian of the Guts asked me a riddle and I couldn't get it. So it sent me here."

"Bummer," says Jake.

Clik shrugs. "It's not so bad. All kinds of stuff comes down here. I use it to make inventions."

He points to a pile of cool-looking gadgets and stuff. Finn is curious.

"Cool!" he says.

The robot eyes Finn's wooden sword. "Perhaps we could trade? Your sword is quite awesome."

"Aw, it's just a crummy play sword," Finn says.

"Then you will not mind trading it," Clik says.

"Hmm. Maybe not," Finn says. "Whatcha got?"

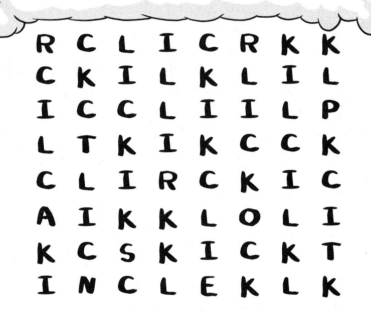

SOLVE THE PUZZLE TO HELP FINN DECIDE WHICH INVENTION TO TAKE

Cross out all the letters that appear in the word *Clik*. Then unscramble the remaining letters to figure out which invention Finn should take.

R C L I C R K K
C K I L K L I L
I C C L I I L P
L T K I K C C K
C L I R C K I C
A I K K L O L I
K C S K I C K T
I N C L E K L K

If Finn takes the transponder, **TURN TO PAGE 119**

If Finn takes the transporter, **TURN TO PAGE 94**

WATcH oUT FoR
wIZARD MAGIC!

"We've got to hurry!" LSP says.

She and Princess Bubblegum make their way to the library. It's an enormous building. Inside, there are rows and rows and rows of bookshelves that are arranged to form a labyrinth. There are books from long ago, and books that were just written, and maybe even a book written in the future.

They go inside, and it's super quiet in there, like always. There's a hush over the whole place pretty much all the time. It's a library thing.

Except now.

"TURTLE PRINCESS!" LSP yells.

But there's no Turtle Princess in sight.

"TURTLE PRINCESS!" LSP yells again.

Then Turtle Princess emerges from one of the rows. She's a green turtle with long blond hair and a cool princess tiara, and she walks on two legs. She's putting one hand to her mouth to shush LSP, and in the other hand she's holding a glowing purple ball.

"Shhh, LSP," she says. "This is a library."

"Of course I know it's a library!" LSP says. "That's why we're here. I need a book and it's super important! Tell her, Princess Bubblegum."

But PB is distracted by the glowing purple ball.

"What's that, Turtle Princess?" she asks.

"Oh, this," Turtle Princess replies. "I found it in the Magic section. There was a wizard here this morning, and he must have dropped it."

PB snorts. "Magic! There's no such thing as magic. Everything magic can be explained by science. Let me see that."

Turtle Princess hands over the glowing ball. Princess Bubblegum places it on one of the tables and takes a magnifying lens from her pocket.

"Interesting," she says. "There must be a power source inside. I'd love to take it apart back in my lab."

Turtle Princess wrings her hands. "Oh no. I've got to put it in the lost and found. That's what I do with everything that gets left behind."

She motions toward a big cardboard box by her desk. It's overflowing with all kinds of junk. A guitar, a wizard's wand, a pair of fuzzy dice.

"Whatever!" LSP cries, and she grabs the ball and throws it into the box. "Bubblegum, have you forgotten that we need to save my parents?"

"Of course not," Princess Bubblegum says. "Turtle Princess, we need a book on black holes."

"Black holes," repeats the Turtle Princess slowly. "Now, let me see. It could be in the Astronomy section. Or the section on Planets and Other Stuff. Or Space. Or History of Holes. Or . . ."

While Turtle Princess rattles on, something weird is happening in the lost and found bin. The ball has opened up, and a purple mist is floating out of it. It snakes around the rows and rows and rows of books. Then it grows tendrils that slide into all the books. But the princesses don't notice because they're all busy talking.

"So you don't know where it is?" LSP finally asks, interrupting Turtle Princess.

"Well, I know where it might be," Turtle Princess says. "Astronomy, or Planets and Other Stuff, or . . ."

"Come on, PB!" Lumpy Space Princess says, dragging her friend away by the arm. "We'll find it on our own!"

"But we have to narrow down our search, or we'll be looking forever," Princess Bubblegum reminds her.

★ ★ You earn 63 ADVENTURE MINUTES. ★ ★

HELP LSP AND PB FIND THE BOOK ON BLACK HOLES

Help LSP and PB navigate the maze of the library. What section will you end up in?

If they go to the A-M section,
TURN TO PAGE 28

If they go to the N-Z section,
TURN TO PAGE 42

DOES A CAGED PRINCESS SING?

LSP tosses the creature into the tank, and she and PB hide. Then a witch enters the room. She's got blue skin and star-shaped eyes and long black hair. She notices the misplaced creature right away.

"Who's been messing with my beasts?" she shrieks. "Comet Temoc!"

Poof! LSP and PB are transported from their hiding place, and now they're right in front of the witch.

"Intruders!" she cries. "I knew it! How convenient. I could use some princesses in my collection. Tardis Sidrat!"

Poof! LSP and PB are trapped in a cage. The witch cackles and leaves the menagerie.

"Get us out of here, PB!" LSP demands.

PB is examining the lock. "Hmm. This seems to be a magical seal."

"What? I thought you don't believe in magic! Use science to open it!" LSP says.

"I'll try," says PB. "But I don't know how long it will take."

THE END

END OF
THE PAGE

"'And the day became night,'" Princess Bubblegum says out loud.

Nothing happens. The letters fly away on the wind, but none of the wedding guests seem to notice. They're all too happy celebrating with Lumpy Space Prince.

Suddenly, PB and LSP hear very quiet footsteps behind them, followed by very quiet shouts.

"Intruders! Intruders!"

The shouting is coming from the Pagelings, the secret guardians of the library books. They look like little folded-up pieces of paper. Paper Pete, the leader, confronts PB and LSP.

"I am Paper Pete, leader of the Pagelings! You do not have permission to be inside this book. You are invaders!"

PB tries to explain that it was a mistake, and LSP starts to ask for help, but the Pagelings won't listen. They sentence the two invaders to spend two thousand pages in a boring book about the history of paper.

"Worst day ever!" cries LSP.

THE END

LUMPY SPACE
WITCH?

Lumpy Space Princess morphs her lumps until she looks like a loaf of bread.

"Oh my glob! Carbs! No!" yells witch-Melissa.

"That's it, witch!" LSP yells. "I won the duel. Now admit it!"

Astrid transforms back into her own form. "All right. You win," she says gloomily.

"Now get Brad out of jail!" LSP demands.

They go back to the cells, and Astrid uses a spell to open up the cell of the real Brad.

"Thanks, LSP," Brad says.

"You're welcome, Brad, even though you're dating my best friend, Melissa," she replies. Then LSP turns to the Space Witch. "Now get those Lumpy Space People out of your stupid monster."

Astrid's starry eyes flash. "You know, I don't like being ordered around by a nonmagical lump like you!" she says. "Maybe I'll just put you all back in prison."

"You will not!" says LSP.

"Will too!" says Astrid.

"Will not!" says LSP.

"Will too!" says Astrid.

"WILL NOT!" LSP yells, and then she punches that witch

because she's so mad. The witch goes down.

"That's more like it," says Jake.

LSP eyes the witch's rocket broom. "I'll just do it myself!"

She hops on the broom and flies through the prison until she finds an open way out. Then she flies to the monster.

"Hey, you!" LSP yells.

The monster looks at her with his big yellow eyes.

"COUGH UP THOSE LUMPY SPACE PEOPLE NOW!" LSP says, and, like, magic sparks fly from her hands. Maybe she's getting power from the rocket broom. She's not sure why, but she doesn't care—it feels awesome.

The monster looks afraid. He obeys and coughs up all the Lumpy Space People. LSP waves to her mom and dad as they tumble out. Everyone lands safely on the land lumps below.

LSP flies back to the prison.

"Hop on," she tells Finn, Jake, and Brad. "I'll get you guys out of here and drop you off."

"What do you mean, drop us off?" asks Finn. "Aren't you coming back to Ooo?"

"Maybe someday, but not today," says LSP. "I'm going to try being Lumpy Space Witch for a while. It's lumping awesome!"

THE END

MORE STUFF TO FIGHT

"LSP, keep talking!" Finn urges.

"Why do you want me to keep talking? That is so stupid. I am not going to keep talking just because you ask me to, Finn!" LSP yells.

Even though LSP is complaining about talking, she's still talking. The sound of her voice makes the bacteria slide away. She follows Finn and Jake as they weave through the bacteria and leave the chamber.

Whoosh! They slide down another squishy tube.

Squoosh! They land in another chamber. It's empty.

"WHERE ARE MY PARENTS?" LSP fumes.

Then more creatures come marching into the chamber. They're in neat lines, like soldiers. These guys are bright green and flat, like plates. They've got little hairy things sticking out of their edges. Like the bacteria, they've got faces.

"Green blood cells?" Jake guesses.

"LSP, yell something and see if it makes them go away," Finn quickly suggests.

"WHY DO YOU KEEP ASKING ME TO YELL THINGS?" LSP yells.

But her voice doesn't do anything to the green cells. They march forward, chanting.

"Attack the invaders! Attack the invaders! Attack the invaders!"

Pow! Jake tries another punch, but his fist just bounces off the gloop.

"Finn, whatcha got in your backpack?" he asks.

Finn rummages through. "Um, a comic book. Some bubble gum. Cheese in a can. A seashell . . ."

"Cheese in a can! That stuff is, like, yummy," LSP yells. "It helps me keep my lumps extra lumpy."

"Throw it to me!" Jake yells.

Finn tosses it. Jake catches it and shakes it. Then he squirts some at one of the cells.

The cheese is a crazy orange color. It hits the cell, and the cell absorbs it. The cheese starts to spread all over it and then . . . *blam!* The cell explodes. Green and orange slimy stuff spews everywhere.

"Awesome!" Finn cries. "Hit 'em all!"

Jake shakes the can. "It's only half full. I have to make sure I don't run out. Can you count these guys for me so I know how much cheese to squirt each time?"

★ ★   **You earn 21 ADVENTURE MINUTES.**   ★ ★

HELP JAKE COUNT THE CELLS!

Count the number of cells on the next page. Make sure you count correctly, or Jake won't have enough cheese to destroy them all!

If you think there are between 40 and 45 cells,
TURN TO PAGE 15

If you think there are between 35 and 39 cells,
TURN TO PAGE 71

THE BoTTOMLESS
BOTTOM

"A telephone?" guesses LSP.

"What the heck is a telephone?" the Tree Witch says. "The answer is a TREE, of course!"

"I was going to guess that," PB says, wishing she had spoken up sooner.

"And that means you lose!" the Tree Witch cackles. Then she turns around, and the princesses see that she is hollow on the bottom, like a hollow tree log.

"Later!" says PB, and she rushes off.

But LSP is not as fast. The Tree Witch starts to suck her up into her bottomless bottom.

"PB, get back here!" LSP demands.

"I'll come back for you!" PB promises.

LSP hopes she'll be back soon!

THE END

NOW, THAT'S A SWEET SOUL!

"I think I know where the jar is," LSP says. She floats down the rows and rows of jars, and stops in front of one.

Inside the jar, is a shining light the color of a blue morning sky on a spring day. It's so pretty to look at that LSP sheds a tear.

"Wow, it's so beautiful," says LSP, moved.

"Let's open it already," says Finn.

"Wait!" says Jake. "Should we, like, find the witch and make her drink it or something?"

Finn looks at the light. "It's her soul, dude. That's a big deal. It's going to go back where it belongs." He's not sure how he knows that, but he just does. Maybe 'cause Finn's soul is pretty sweet, too.

Jake shrugs. "Okay, then."

LSP opens the jar. The blue light floats out. It hangs in the air a minute, then floats to the back of the room. Another door opens, and the light passes through it.

"Follow it!" Finn yells.

They chase after the blue light as it goes all twisty and turny through the witch's lair. The light goes through a door, and there's the witch, standing in some kind of control room or something.

"What is—" she starts to say, and then the light just flies

into her open mouth! Astrid's angry look slowly melts. And then she's smiling.

"Oh my goodness," she says. "You found my Sweet Soul, did you?"

"Yes!" says LSP. "And I hope you're lumping nice now. Because you, like, captured us, and your monster is out there eating everybody up."

"Sorry about that," says Astrid. "And I'd better fix it fast, because if I know myself, I'll be taking out my Sweet Soul again. It's no fun being good all the time."

"Then do it!" orders LSP.

"Cool your jets," says Astrid. "Now, let me see. I know. I'll cast a spell to undo all the bad stuff I did. Hold your horses. It's a big one!"

Astrid's star-shaped eyes flash. Blue light sparkles on the ends of her fingertips.

"Bolide, Corona, Parralax!" she says. "Edilob, Anoroc, Xalarrap!"

Boom! Blue light explodes all over the place.

LSP floats up to Finn and Jake. Finn is fooling around with a wooden sword. Jake is playing the violin.

"Hey, LSP," Finn says. "What's up?"

LSP stops. She was sure she had a reason to see Finn and Jake— but now she can't remember. Weird! None of them can remember. It's the witch's spell.

"I don't lumping know!" LSP says, and then she floats away.

★★ **You earn 37 ADVENTURE MINUTES.** ★★

THE END

EVERY STORY
NEEDS AN ENDING

Princess Bubblegum jumps out from behind the ice sculpture.

"Hey, over here!" she yells.

The Ice Queen spins at the sound of PB's voice. PB is already running toward another ice sculpture. By the time the Ice Queen shoots an icy blast, PB is safe behind it. The blast hits the sculpture, and ricochets back to the Ice Queen.

Boom! The Ice Queen shatters into icy pieces. Her attack has backfired.

A cheer goes up from the wedding guests. That may sound mean, but the Ice Queen was really awful. Lumpy Space Prince floats up to them.

"Like, thank you, whoever you are," he says.

LSP turns to Princess Bubblegum. "This is awesome," she says. "Now Lumpy Space Prince doesn't have to marry her."

PB frowns. "Yes, but that means the story won't end, and we'll be stuck here forever."

LSP looks around. The wedding guests are all cheering and dancing. With the mean Ice Queen gone, most of their troubles are over. It's a world with no Ice Queen—and no Ice King, either.

"Maybe it won't be so bad," LSP says.

THE END

FREE
THE BEASTS!

LSP floats in front of the middle cell.

"Nebula Aluben!" she cries, repeating the witch's spell. The bars slide open.

"Oh, Brad!" LSP cries, hugging him.

"Uh, hey, baby," he says.

"Dude, do you know the way out of here?" Finn asks.

Brad nods. "Sure. Follow me."

They hurry through the twisty, turny halls of the prison. Finally, Brad stops in front of a big metal door. He opens it and steps inside, and the others follow.

"Whoa," Finn says, looking around.

The room is filled with cages, big ones and small ones. Inside the cages are all kinds of weird-looking creatures. A two-headed golden bird. A snake with legs. A green, fluffy thing with two big eyes.

"This isn't the way out," LSP says.

"I know," says Brad. "And I'm not Brad."

Brad's body starts to, like, shimmer and stuff. Then he doesn't look like Brad anymore. He looks like a pudgy white dude, like he's made out of bread dough or something.

"What have you done with Brad?" LSP demands.

"I didn't do anything," says not-Brad. "The witch captured

him and put him in prison. When I saw you were looking for him, I shape-shifted into him."

"So you're a shape-shifter," Finn says, poking his soft body. "Cool."

"My real name is Miguel," the guy says.

"Are you lumping kidding me?" LSP fumes. "I was supposed to save Brad, not you!"

Miguel shimmers again and shape-shifts back into Brad. "But I had to get out of there! All these guys are my friends. And the witch has kept them locked up in here for years."

He waves a hand at all the strange creatures in their cages.

"So let's just set 'em free," Jake says.

"There's a spell on the cages," Miguel says. "The witch figured out that I was on to her spells, so she moved me from the menagerie into the prison."

"What's the spell?" Finn asks.

"I hid it in a note in case Astrid found it," Miguel says, showing them a piece of paper.

★ ✹   **You earn 50 ADVENTURE MINUTES.**   ★ ✹

HELP THE GANG FIGURE OUT THE SPELL

Read the note. The letters that make up the words to the spell are hidden in this note. Here's a clue: These letters are real beginners!

Never give up! Astrid cannot keep you here forever. Don't get discouraged. If you do, get back up again. Right will win in the end. Risks will reward you. In the end, you'll succeed. Destiny awaits you. After all is said and done, you'll get out of here. Now go do it!

If the spell is NADIR RIDAN, **TURN TO PAGE 117**

If the spell is NEVER GIVE UP, **TURN TO PAGE 82**

TAMiNG
THE MONSTER

LSP leads everyone up through the tube on the right. It leads into the monster's giant mouth. It's dark, though, because the mouth is closed.

"Oh no! We're trapped!" LSP cries.

"Maybe not," says Jake. He reaches up with his arm and tickles the uvula of the monster. *Uvula* is a weird word, but it just means that thing that dangles down in the back of your throat. Luckily, the monster has a uvula, too.

Jake makes the monster gag. The monster's mouth opens wide and he coughs up LSP and Jake and Finn and all the Lumpy Space People. They land on the big land lump where the Lumpy Space King and Queen live.

"See? I told you I would rescue you," LSP says. "Now can I borrow the car?"

Before her parents can answer, the monster makes a loud groaning sound. It's so loud, it makes the land lump shake. Now they can see what the monster looks like. It's, like, a big, black blob floating through space, with round yellow eyes and a big mouth.

"I think it's gonna try to suck us up again!" Finn cries.

"I ain't going back inside that squishy beast," Jake says.

LSP is listening hard. "Oh my glob, I think I understand!

The monster is hungry because it's sad. I know because I get hungry whenever I'm sad. And I'm sad all the time."

"Why would a monster be sad?" Melissa asks.

"You know, I think I saw a meteor or some junk sticking out of the side of it when it coughed us up," Finn says. "Maybe it's hurt."

"It stinks to be sad and hungry," says LSP. She turns to her parents. "Mom, Dad, I'm getting in that car and I'm going to help that monster!"

"No offense, LSP, but that might be a better job for heroes like us," Finn says.

★ ★   **You earn 77 ADVENTURE MINUTES.**   ★ ★

WHO SHOULD HELP THE MONSTER?

On the next page, color in the shapes with two dots inside to find out who should go help the monster. Remember, heroes come in all shapes and sizes!

Please see instructions on previous page.

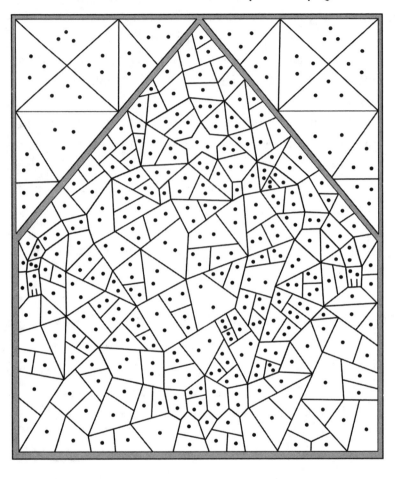

If you think LSP should help the monster,
TURN TO PAGE 86

If you think Jake should help the monster,
TURN TO PAGE 39

MORE ADVENTURE?

"'And they danced all night,'" Princess Bubblegum reads aloud, and then *whoosh*! They're out of the book and back in the library. Finn and Jake are standing there.

"What are you doing here?" LSP asks.

"We rescued everybody," Finn says matter-of-factly. "We heard you were here, so we thought you'd want to know."

"Thank you," says PB.

"And now I'm bored again," says Finn. "I wish I had another adventure to go on."

"Well, the Ice Queen got out of a book and now she's wandering around Ooo," says PB.

"Shmowzow!" exclaims Finn. "The Ice Queen from Ice King's dumb fan fiction? She's super evil and junk. Sounds like we've got another adventure."

Finn, Jake, PB, and LSP leave the library. But LSP heads away from the others.

"LSP, aren't you coming to help us?" PB asks.

"I've got problems of my own, remember?" LSP asks. "I've got to make my parents let me borrow the car!"

★ ★ **You earn 53 ADVENTURE MINUTES.** ★ ★

THE END

69

SPIDER
FOOD!

Finn is slashing at the spiders, but he keeps hitting the hologram ones instead of the real ones.

The real spiders are squirting this yellow junk at everybody. Jake slips and falls in it. LSP is freaked out by it.

"Gross!" she yells. She grabs Brad and pulls him in front of her, like a lumpy shield. "Brad, you tried to save me. How romantic!"

Brad tries to argue. "But I—" *Splat!* Yellow spider goo hits him in the face.

Then the real spiders start shooting out webby stuff. It wraps around Finn, Jake, LSP, and Brad like cocoons. They struggle to break out of the webs, but they're super-duper strong.

"What do we do now?" LSP wails.

"I don't know what we do," Jake says. "But I know what those spiders are gonna do. They're gonna eat us!"

THE END

THIs LuMPiNG
STINKS!

Jake squirts the green cells with the cheese. They get past most of them. But then Jake tries to squirt another one—and nothing comes out.

"Uh-oh," says Jake.

The rest of the green cells swarm them. They push against them with their sticky bodies and march them down another tube. Then they push Finn, Jake, and LSP out of the monster's ear!

The three of them go floating through space. They're not anywhere near land lumps, and there's no gravity. Even Lumpy Space Princess can't hang out in space without gravity.

"This is really bad!" yells Finn.

"This lumping stinks!" yells LSP as they all go spiraling away. "I never should have jumped into that black hole with you guys."

THE END

THE LUMPY
SPACE STOMACH

"Correct!" says the Guardian of the Guts. "Well done!"

Then he points to one of the tube tunnels. "You will find your people down that way, Lumpy One."

"Why couldn't you just tell us in the first place?" LSP complains, and then she heads down the tunnel.

Before he follows LSP, Finn turns to the Candy Corn Dude.

"Are you sure you don't want us to get you loose?" he asks.

"And leave my post? Never!" the Guardian replies.

With a shrug, Finn jumps down the tube after LSP, and Jake is right behind him. At the end of the tube is a flap. LSP shoots through the flap, and then Finn and Jake do, too.

"Whoa!" Finn yells as he finds himself in midair. Below him is a bubbling sea of acid-looking stuff. All the Lumpy Space People are there, floating safely above it. But Finn is about to splash right in!

"Gotcha!" Jake yells. He's gripping onto the fleshy wall with one hand and grabbing Finn with the other.

"Thanks, dude," Finn says.

The fleshy wall has bumps in it, kind of like ledges, so Finn and Jake can perch on one without falling into the acid below.

"I think we're in the stomach of whatever monster this is," Jake guesses.

"It's a good thing those lumpy people can float, or else

they'd be digested right now," Finn points out.

There are dozens of Lumpy Space People hanging out in the giant stomach. Mostly, they're just freaking out. Their voices echo around the stomach.

"This is so lame!"

"Somebody get us out of here!"

"What the lump is going on?"

LSP zips around, searching for her parents. Then she spots them.

"Mom! Dad!" she cries, and floats up to them.

Lumpy Space King and Lumpy Space Queen are purple, like their daughter. Because they're married, they are joined into one big, lumpy cloud with two heads and two crowns and four arms.

"Princess! Are you all right?" Lumpy Space Queen asks.

"I'm more than all right. I've come to rescue you," Lumpy Space Princess says. "Even though I'm still mad that you wouldn't lend me the stupid car!"

"This is no time to talk about a car," Lumpy Space King scolds.

Then a pink, lumpy girl with big, wide eyes floats up. It's Melissa, LSP's best friend.

"LSP! You're here!" Melissa says.

"Hello, Melissa," LSP says. Even though Melissa is her best friend, it's kind of complicated, because Melissa is dating Brad. And Brad is LSP's old boyfriend. Deep down, she still has feelings for Brad.

"Did you bring Finn and Jake with you?" Melissa asks.

"Of course I did. They're up there." LSP points up to the stomach wall. Finn and Jake wave.

"So where's Brad?" LSP asks.

Melissa's big eyes get teary. "I don't know. I can't find him anywhere."

"Brad is missing? Oh my glob!" LSP wails. "I mean, not that I care or anything."

Lumpy Space King interrupts. "So, what about this rescue, Princess?"

"Stop bugging me!" LSP says. "I just got here."

Then she floats up to Finn and Jake. "So, can we get everyone out of here now?"

"Sure," Finn says. "But I don't get it. Why doesn't everybody just float out?"

"Because that flap only opens one way," Lumpy Space King explains, pointing up to the tube. "We can't get it open."

"No problem," Finn says. He climbs up the fleshy stomach wall to the flap. He tries to open it, but LSK is right—it won't budge. Finn tries to pry it open with his sword, but he can only get it open a tiny bit.

"I've got it from here," Jake says. He stretches out his arm and flattens it and slides it under the flap. Then he pushes the flap open from the other side.

Lumpy Space Princess calls out to her people.

"Everybody, come on! I'm rescuing you!"

Jake holds the flap open while LSP leads all the Lumpy Space People up through the tube. Then Jake and Finn climb up after them. It's a lot harder than floating, and the tube is slippery. When they get to the top, there's a whole crowd of Lumpy Space People blocking the way out.

"What's the hang-up?" Jake asks LSP after he and Finn

push their way through the crowd.

"There's, like, two tubes we have to choose from," LSP says. "I don't know which way is out."

★ ★ You earn 101 ADVENTURE MINUTES. ★ ★

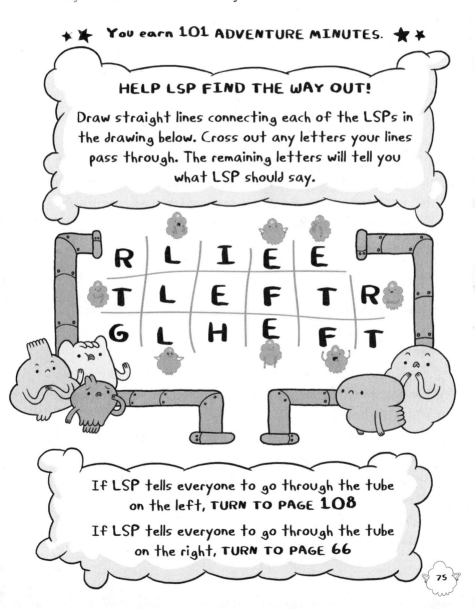

HELP LSP FIND THE WAY OUT!

Draw straight lines connecting each of the LSPs in the drawing below. Cross out any letters your lines pass through. The remaining letters will tell you what LSP should say.

R L I E E
T L E F T R
G L H E F T

If LSP tells everyone to go through the tube on the left, **TURN TO PAGE 108**

If LSP tells everyone to go through the tube on the right, **TURN TO PAGE 66**

OH MY GLOB!
IT'S BRAD!

"Nebula Aluben!" LSP reads aloud when she solves the code.

The gate to their cell magically slides open.

"It was a spell!" Finn realizes. "Awesome. Let's get out of here."

They hurry out of the cell. They're in a long hallway with cold gray walls. They head down the hallway and then make a left into another hall, and then a right, and then a left again—the place is, like, a crazy maze! The whole time, they're passing lots of empty prison cells.

Then LSP skids to a stop. "Oh my glob! It's Brad!"

Brad is hanging out in one of the cells. The reason LSP is freaked is because he is her ex-boyfriend. They used to eat chili fries together. Then Brad tried to kiss her on the mouth, and it was too intense for LSP, so they broke up.

LSP has complicated feelings for Brad. He and her best friend, Melissa, started dating, and she's kind of jealous. Deep down, she still really likes him.

And now, here in the middle of space, inside the Space Witch's prison, is Brad. He doesn't look much like other Lumpy Space People, but he is one. For one thing, he has legs and he can't float. And he's not super lumpy. He's blue, and the top of his head is kind of flat. His eyes always look half closed, like he's bored or something.

"Brad, what are you doing here?" LSP asks.

"That Space Witch kidnapped me," Brad says in his flat voice. "She says I'm gonna help her take care of her pets."

"Well, I'm gonna rescue you, Brad!" LSP cries. She looks at the paper. She knows if she says the spell aloud, the gate will open.

"LSP, over here!"

"LSP, over here!"

The voices come out of nowhere. LSP looks from side to side—there's a Brad in the cell to the left of Brad. There's a Brad in the cell to the right of Brad.

"It's a Triple Brad Brain Buster!" Finn cries.

Which one is the real Brad?

★ ✭ **You earn 19 ADVENTURE MINUTES.** ✭ ★

HELP LSP FIND THE REAL BRAD!

Turn the page to help LSP find the real Brad.
If she frees the wrong Brad, who knows
what will happen?

Two of these Brads are exactly alike.
The one that is different is the real Brad.

If you choose the Brad on the left, **TURN TO PAGE 36**

If you choose the Brad in the middle, **TURN TO PAGE 63**

If you choose the Brad on the right, **TURN TO PAGE 7**

TO THE
BLACK HOLE!

"You're right!" says Cuber. "It's *A-E-I-O-U*! Abracadaniel had an accordion. Engagement Ring Princess kissed an elephant. The Ice Cube guy had an ice-cream cone. Old Lady Princess lost her orange opticals. And Ursula was in an underwear shop. I'll see you crimpy glimmers on the triode flippin' the diode!"

Suddenly, they're back in the library.

"We did it!" PB exclaims. "Now let's find that book on black holes and go save your parents."

"It's about time!" says LSP.

They find the book, say good-bye to Turtle Princess, and head to the portal that leads to Lumpy Space. Once they get there, the black hole is gone, and the Lumpy Space People are floating around. Then they see Finn and Jake.

"Hey, LSP and PB," Finn says. "So, Jake and I fixed everything and saved everybody. You know, hero stuff."

"My parents!" LSP cries, and floats away to find them.

★ ★ **You earn 20 ADVENTURE MINUTES.** ★ ★

THE END

T Is for
TREE WITCH

LSP puts the creature in the correct tank. Then she and PB find a sweet hiding place. They hold their breath as they hear the Space Witch enter.

They don't dare look. They hear her sniffing around, but she seems satisfied that everything is okay.

"Dratted malfunctioning alarm," they hear her mutter. And then she leaves.

"That was close!" says LSP. "So what do we do now?"

PB leaves the hiding spot and goes to the port in the wall. "We get out, and that should get us to the next witch. I'm guessing that since the witch types are alphabetical, we'll be seeing the Tree Witch."

PB pushes open the port and climbs through. LSP follows her. Turns out, Princess Bubblegum was right (but isn't she always, almost?). Instead of spiraling off into endless space, they find themselves back in Ooo, in a dark forest. There's a tree in front of them with long blond hair that looks a lot like Finn's hair. Wait, a tree with hair?

The tree opens its bright green eyes, and they suddenly realize they're looking at the Tree Witch. Her skin is like bark, and she's got a branch for a nose.

"Ooh, princesses," she says. "Fun! I've got an idea. I'll give you a riddle. If you get it right, I'll let you leave the forest."

"And if we get it wrong?" asks PB.

"Then I'll suck you up into my bottomless bottom!" cackles the Tree Witch, and that sounds really nasty. But PB is not afraid.

"What's the riddle?" asks PB.

"What has no fingers but many rings?" asks the Tree Witch.

★ ★ You earn 89 ADVENTURE MINUTES. ★ ★

CAN YOU HELP LSP AND PB SOLVE THE RIDDLE TO GET PAST THE TREE WITCH?

If you think the answer is "a tree," TURN TO PAGE 102

If you think the answer is "a telephone," TURN TO PAGE 59

BEASTLY!

"Never give up!" Miguel shouts. Then he starts to shimmer. Fur sprouts all over his body. Horns pop out of his head.

"Why are you shape-shifting right now?" LSP asks.

"I'm not doing it!" Miguel cries. "And you guys are, too!"

"What?" LSP wails.

She looks down at her lumps. They're covered with feathers. She can feel a beak growing on her face. She's too freaked out to think of anybody else, but if she looked around, she would see that Finn is now a bug with a hard shell and lots of extra legs, and Jake is a fluffy sheep with two arms growing from his back.

"What the math? That spell turned us into beasts!" Finn says.

Jake claps the hands on his back. "Yeah, man, look. I could play two violins at once."

Then Astrid bursts in. "So you tried to free my pets, did you? And look where it got you! Ha!"

She quickly puts them in her magic cages. Then Astrid leaves the menagerie and locks the door behind her.

"This is lumping ridiculous!" LSP fumes. "Miguel, get us out of here!"

"I can't shape-shift anymore," Miguel says.

LSP sighs. "I wish I had rescued the *real* Brad instead!"

THE END

IT'S LUMPY
SPACE PRINCE!

The penguin motions for LSP and PB to pass. Their pieced-together ticket has worked!

They head up the icy stairs to the castle. Lots of residents from the Candy Kingdom are there. The entrance to the castle is a big arch cut into the ice. They go through it into a huge, icy room.

The room is decorated with giant ice sculptures of the Ice Queen. A penguin band is playing snappy music. Penguin servers are passing out bubbly drinks.

"This is quite a celebration," Princess Bubblegum says.

"It's all from the Ice King's imagination!" LSP reminds her. "I wonder what sucker has agreed to marry the Ice Queen in this story?"

The room suddenly gets quiet.

"I guess we'll find out," says PB.

The penguins play a wedding march, and the Ice Queen slowly comes down the stairs. Now, Ice King is a pretty gross-looking dude. He's got a long, white, nasty beard, and his toenails are gnarly. But in the fan fiction he writes, the Ice Queen is super gorgeous. She's got long icy-blue tresses and cool lightning-shaped eyebrows, and she wears a beautiful blue gown.

She's also way smarter and meaner than Ice King. Already, her ice-blue eyes are suspiciously scanning the crowd.

"We'd better not let her see us," PB whispers. She motions to LSP, and they duck behind one of the ice sculptures.

Then the groom comes down the opposite staircase. He's lumpy and purple. In fact, he looks almost exactly like Lumpy Space Princess with a mustache.

"Lumpy Space Prince!" LSP gasps. It was always weird hearing Ice King tell stories about the male version of herself. But it's even weirder seeing him in person like this.

"All right, everybody!" the Ice Queen shouts. "It's time for the wedding to begin. So be quiet!"

LSP can't help herself. "Lumpy Space Prince can't marry the Ice Queen! That would be terrible."

"It's just a story, LSP," PB reminds her in a whisper. "We need to see this to get through the end."

"No way!" LSP yells. She floats out from behind the sculpture. "Stop this wedding right now!"

The Ice Queen turns around, her eyes flashing. "Who dares interrupt my wedding?" She spots LSP. "Who are you?"

"I'm Lumpy Space Princess, and this wedding is over!" LSP shouts.

The Ice Queen points at LSP, and an icy blast shoots from her fingers. LSP ducks, and the blast hits the ice sculpture. It cracks the sculpture, then ricochets off and almost hits the Ice Queen, but she dodges out of the way.

"Hmm," says PB. "I think I know how we can get out of this."

★ ★ You earn 34 ADVENTURE MINUTES. ★ ★

HELP PB AND LSP BATTLE THE ICE QUEEN

PB needs to find an ice sculpture just like the one that was hit. Compare the four ice sculptures to the original. Which one is an exact match?

If you think the exact match is #2 or #4, **TURN TO PAGE 62**

If you think the exact match is #1 or #3, **TURN TO PAGE 103**

LSP To
THE RESCUE

"You can't stop me, Finn! I'm going up there!" LSP insists. "And, Mom and Dad, I'm borrowing the car!"

LSP floats over to the car and hops into the driver's seat. She revs the engine and then zooms up into space toward the monster.

The monster is big and blobby and scary. But LSP isn't thinking about that. She's thinking about how hungry she is and how good a cheeseburger would taste right about now. And how lame it must be to float around in outer space, where there are no cheeseburgers. And how it must stink to have a meteor sticking out of you. Like how sometimes when she eats popcorn, it gets stuck in her lumps. That's no fun at all.

"I'm coming to help you, monster!" she cries.

One of the monster's big yellow eyes sees her, and then it starts to open its mouth. Is it going to eat her?

But LSP is close to the meteor now. Finn was right—it's totally stuck in the monster's blobby body. The meteor is about as big as the car. No problem!

Vroooom! LSP accelerates and slams into the meteor! The car knocks the big rock out of the monster's body. The meteor goes spiraling away.

"I hope you feel better now," LSP tells the monster. "And

if you're not sad anymore, then please stop trying to eat us, all right?"

Does the monster understand Lumpy Space language? Maybe, and maybe not. But it is definitely happy that the meteor is gone. It closes its mouth and smiles at LSP. And then it floats away.

LSP drives the car back down to the land lump. All the Lumpy Space People gather around her, cheering.

"Nice job, LSP," says Finn.

"That was so not lame," adds Melissa.

LSP's parents float up. "We are super lumping proud of you, daughter," says Lumpy Space King.

"Does that mean you'll let me borrow the car?" asks LSP.

"No," he replies.

"What the lump? No?" LSP fumes.

Her dad smiles. "We are so proud that we will buy you your very own car," he says.

"Awesome!" LSP says. "Just don't get me something lame, okay?"

★ ★ You earn 53 ADVENTURE MINUTES. ★ ★

THE END

HERe cOME THE PAGELINGS!

The penguin looks at the ticket Princess Bubblegum hands him. Then he scowls and pokes at PB angrily. A bunch of other penguins waddle up and push them away from the castle.

"I guess that didn't work," LSP says. "This is so lame! We'll be stuck in this book forever!"

"I'm sure we can figure out another way to get into that wedding," Princess Bubblegum says. "I don't consider a bunch of penguins to be worthy opponents."

The angry penguins *wenk* at them and waddle away.

"So what now?" LSP asks.

Suddenly, they hear a voice behind them.

"Intruders! Stop!"

They turn and see that the voice belongs to a folded-up piece of paper. He's with three other folded-up pieces of paper. LSP and PB don't know it, but these guys are the Pagelings. They are the secret guardians of the books in the library. Finn and Jake met them once.

The Pagelings all look different. Their leader, and the one who does all the talking, is Paper Pete. He's folded into a triangle with legs, arms, and a paper sword. The others are folded into the shape of a horse, a cute little guy with a crown, and a bat-like dude.

"Who are you?" Princess Bubblegum asks.

"I am Paper Pete, leader of the Pagelings," Pete says. "We guard the books in this library. And you two definitely are not part of this book. You must be invaders!"

"We come in peace," says PB.

"Yeah, we got sucked in here by a magic wizard's ball," says LSP. "It's totally not our fault."

"Then we will help you get out," Paper Pete says. "Just grab on."

LSP takes Paper Pete's hand, and PB holds on to the wing of the bat dude. Then *whoosh*! They fly right out of the book.

"Awesome!" cries LSP. "Now we can find that book on black holes and save my parents!"

"No, we would love to show you another book," says Paper Pete. "It's very special. It's from the future."

"We don't have time for that!" LSP yells, but Paper Pete isn't listening.

TURN TO PAGE 20

NO
DEAL!

"I will not make a deal with you, witch!" LSP says firmly. "I will never give up my love for Brad! Never!"

Astrid shrugs. "Fine. I'll just send you back to your stupid land lump so Carl can eat you right up."

"Who's Carl?" LSP asks.

"That big monster out there, you dolt!" yells Astrid. "Enough! Kelvin Nivlek!"

Bam! In an instant, they're all back in Lumpy Space. Jake, Finn, and Brad are confused because they just got unfrozen.

LSP floats to Brad. "Oh, Brad! That witch wanted me to give up the part of my heart that loves you. But I can't, I just can't!"

Up above them, the monster is starting to open its mouth.

"Um, LSP, that's nice and all, but I'm dating Melissa, remember?" Brad asks.

"Are you serious? After I rescued you and everything?" LSP fumes. "Well, forget it, Brad. I don't love you anymore. I was just kidding. And now you're going to help me get rid of that monster!"

TURN TO PAGE **22**

94

UNDERWEAR IS
BETTER THAN HERE

LSP floats away, and PB follows her. Next, they find themselves at the edge of the Ice Kingdom. A little dude who looks like an ice cube is standing there. He's holding an ice-cream cone and crying.

"What's the matter?" PB asks.

"My ice cream is melting!" the Ice Cube guy says between sobs.

"Then go someplace colder!" LSP says impatiently.

"Hey! Good idea!" says the Ice Cube dude, and he skips away toward the icy mountains.

Then Old Lady Princess slowly walks up to them. She's short and really wrinkly.

"Has anyone seen my orange opticals?" she asks.

PB pulls a pair of eyeglasses out of Old Lady Princess's hair.

"Do you mean these?" she asks.

Old Lady Princess grabs them and puts them on. "Much better! I can't see a thing without these." Then she walks away.

LSP groans. "These are the dumbest stories."

"Maybe," says PB. "But we're almost done. And I think I know where to go next."

PB leads LSP into the nearby village and walks into an underwear shop. Inside, they find Ursula, the handmaiden of the Flame Princess. Ursula's flaming hair is throwing sparks on all the racks of underwear. A candy saleslady is frantically running around, trying to put out fires.

"Get out of here right now, before you burn down the place!" she yells.

"This is unfair!" Ursula cries, and storms out.

PB and LSP leave the store, and there is Cuber!

"So you're done, are you? Do you think you know the theme of all five graybles?" he asks.

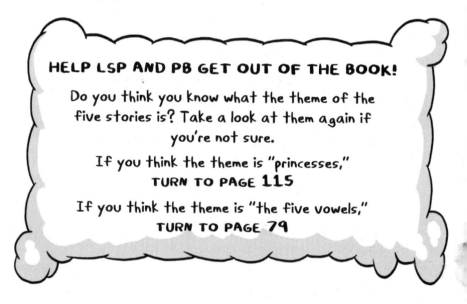

HELP LSP AND PB GET OUT OF THE BOOK!

Do you think you know what the theme of the five stories is? Take a look at them again if you're not sure.

If you think the theme is "princesses,"
TURN TO PAGE 115

If you think the theme is "the five vowels,"
TURN TO PAGE 79

NOT So SWEET . . .

"I think it's this jar," says LSP, floating over to one of the shelves.

She picks up a glass jar. Inside is a bubbling red liquid. Little sparks are shooting up from it.

"That doesn't look like a Sweet Soul," says Finn.

"Of course it is!" says LSP. She opens the lid and . . .

BLAMMO!

THE END

AWESOME
INVENTION!

Clik gives Finn the transporter.

"Thanks," says Finn. "What does it do?"

"It transports," Clik replies.

"Yeah," adds Jake. "What else would it do?"

LSP floats between them. "Can you please stop talking about lame inventions? We need to find my parents!"

Clik points. "The stomach is that way. That's where you'll find them."

"Thanks, dude," Finn says, and they leave Clik waving the sword around like he's battling monsters.

They head down a tube and go through a flap and then they're in the monster's stomach. Jake has to grab onto the sides and then grab Finn so they don't fall into the big pool of stomach acid at the bottom. The Lumpy Space People are floating around, so they're safe.

"Mom! Dad!" LSP cries, and she hugs her parents. "We're here to rescue you."

"How are you going to get us out of here?" Lumpy Space King asks. "You're trapped, too."

"Yeah, but we have an awesome invention," Finn says. "It's a transporter."

"Then transport us out of here, already!" LSP demands.

"You know, it wouldn't hurt you to say please," Jake says.

"If you don't use that transporter now and rescue my parents, I will hurt you!" LSP says angrily. She gets really hyped up when she's upset.

"Fine, fine," says Finn. "I think I just gotta press this button."

He presses a button, and—*poof!*—Finn, Jake, and all the Lumpy Space People inside the monster's stomach disappear. Then they reappear back on the land lumps below.

"We did it!" Jake says.

LSP looks up. "Yeah, whatever. That gross monster is still hanging around up there. We need to make it go away forever!"

LSP floats to her parents' car and jumps in.

"Princess! What are you doing?" Lumpy Space King asks.

LSP ignores him. "Finn and Jake! Are you coming with me?"

"Sure," Finn says. They jump in the car, and LSP speeds toward the monster.

Now they can totally see it's a monster and not a black hole. It's got an enormous round and blobby black body, almost like a small moon. There are these tentacle things sticking out in different places and wiggling. It's eating everything in sight.

"So, how are we gonna attack this thing?" Jake asks.

"I'm not sure yet," Finn says.

Suddenly, they see an orange streak whiz past them.

"What the lump was that?" LSP asks.

TURN TO PAGE 99

LSP VS. THE BACTERIA ARMY

"My luuuuuuuuumps!" LSP yells as she slides down the tube with Finn and Jake.

Squish! They land in another fleshy chamber. There is no sign of the Lumpy Space People.

"This is lame. My parents aren't here!" LSP complains.

Then a cry fills the chamber—but it's not a cry for help. It's a battle cry.

"*Waaaaaaaaaaaaaaaaaah!*"

These neon-blue creatures come streaming in. Each one is as big as LSP. They're round and they've got spikes coming out of them. They look like what some bacteria look like under a microscope, except they're way bigger. And they've got faces.

Jake is psyched. "It's monster-punching time!"

He stretches out his arm and punches the nearest bacteria. His arm just gets stuck inside the bacteria's gooey body. Jake quickly pulls back his arm.

The bacteria charge toward them, waving their spiky things.

Finn goes after one with his sword. At first, it looks like it works. The bacteria splits in half. But then it just gloops right back together.

"Totally gross!" LSP yells. "You guys are so lame! Why can't you fight them?"

As she yells, something weird happens. The bacteria slide away. Their faces are screwed up in pain.

"LSP, say something else," Jake says.

"What good is that, Jake?" LSP fumes. "We should be rescuing my parents!"

The bacteria slide away again. Finn sees what Jake is up to.

"I get it," he says. "LSP's voice repels the bacteria. If she keeps talking, we can get past them."

★ ★ You earn 17 ADVENTURE MINUTES. ★ ★

HELP LSP, JAKE, AND FINN GET PAST THE BACTERIA ARMY

On the next page, start at the arrow. You can move up, down, left, and right. There's only one way out of the chamber. Try to get there without lifting your pencil from the paper. If you hit a bacteria, you fail!

If you make it to the exit, **TURN TO PAGE 56**

If you run into a bacteria, **TURN TO PAGE 24**

ASTRID THE SPACE WITCH

The orange streak loops in the sky and then zooms right toward them! This time, they can see what it's all about.

There's a lady with blue skin riding on a broom. Her weird eyes are shaped like stars, and her long black hair streams behind her. The orange streak is coming out of the back of the broom as she flies.

"It's, like, a Space Witch on a rocket broom!" Finn says.

The witch slows down and circles the car, cackling.

"Get away from my pet!" she shrieks.

Jake looks over at the enormous blobby monster. "That thing is your pet?"

"It's a horrible monster!" LSP yells. She's not afraid of any witch. "And it ate my parents and my friends! So get out of our way so we can fight him!"

Sparks fly out of the witch's star eyes. "Nobody messes with Astrid the Space Witch!" she cries, and then she points at the car. "Albedo Odebla!"

Lasers shoot from her fingertips. It looks super cool, but it's bad news for LSP, Finn, and Jake. The lasers are like magic lassos that grab the car and drag it across space behind the rocket broom.

"Let us go right now!" LSP yells angrily as they fly farther and farther from the monster. But the witch just cackles more loudly.

She flies them toward what looks like a giant meteor floating in space, or maybe it's a small moon. Then they see that there are all these, like, doors and windows in it. Somebody lives there.

"Welcome to my prison!" Astrid announces. She flies through one of the open doors and then they're inside the prison. She dumps the car inside a bare cell with metal bars on the front. Then she slams the door shut.

"See you later. I need to go feed my other pets," Astrid says, and then she flies away.

LSP floats out of the car and shakes the bars. "Let us out, you lumping witch!"

Jake stretches his arm way, way, way out through the bars. Then he brings it back. He's holding a slip of paper.

"What's that, dude?" Finn asks.

"I thought I could swipe the key from her pocket," Jake says. "But all I got was this."

Finn and LSP look at the paper. There's a bunch of letters on it.

"Looks kinda like a secret code," Finn says.

"Give me that!" LSP says, snatching the paper from Jake. "I'm, like, an expert on secrets. When Brittany had a crush on Dylan and she told me not to tell anybody, I only told, like, seven people."

"That actually sounds like you're bad at secrets," Finn points out.

"Whatever!" says LSP.

HELP LSP CRACK THE CODE

Below, use the key on top to turn the letters that make no sense on the bottom into actual words. Get it right and something pretty cool might happen.

KEY

A	B	C	D	E	F	G	H	I	J	K	L	M	N
J	Z	X	Y	U	W	T	V	R	S	P	Q	N	O

O	P	Q	R	S	T	U	V	W	X	Y	Z
L	M	I	K	G	H	E	F	C	D	A	B

MUZEOY YOEZUM

If you think the message is MUZELA ALEZUM,
TURN TO PAGE 40

If you think the message is NEBULA ALUBEN,
TURN TO PAGE 76

101

PRINCESSES TO THE RESCUE

"It's a tree!" PB says quickly.

"Right!" says the Tree Witch. "Guess I'll have to let you pass."

PB and LSP hurry through the forest—and when they get to the end, they're back in the library! They're out of the book!

"Now, let's get to that portal!" says PB.

PB and LSP leave the library and take the portal to Lumpy Space. The black hole is still in the sky, but it's getting smaller.

"So, remember what we learned in the menagerie?" asks PB. "We can control the black hole with two words: Tyson Nosyt!"

"Yeah, what she said!" LSP shouts up at the black sky. "Now cough up everybody in there!"

At first, there's no change. Then the black hole opens up and starts spitting stuff out!

Lots of Lumpy Space People come tumbling out of the hole, back onto the land lumps. Lumpy Space King and Queen land right next to LSP. Then so do Finn and Jake.

"Hey, we did it!" Jake says.

"No, *we* did," LSP corrects him. "Me and Princess Bubblegum. Two princesses. We're the heroes this time."

★ ★ **You earn 160 ADVENTURE MINUTES.** ★ ★

THE END

SOME
ENDING

Princess Bubblegum jumps out from behind an ice sculpture.

"Hey, over here!" she yells.

PB ducks behind another statue. The Ice Queen hits it with another blast. This time, the sculpture completely shatters. Ice Queen flies down and confronts PB and LSP.

"Who are you?" she asks. "And what is that?"

She's pointing to the wizard's ball, which has somehow entered the story. It's glowing with purple magic. The Ice Queen picks it up.

"Wonderful magic!" she says. "A portal to another world, and out of this crummy one! Maybe I'll find a better prince to marry. I'm outta here!"

"Wait, no!" PB cries, but the Ice Queen disappears in a cloud of purple mist.

"Yay! She's not marrying Lumpy Space Prince!" LSP says.

"But the story still needs an ending, or we can't get out," PB says.

Suddenly, they hear somebody cry, "Something's falling from the sky!"

They all rush outside, and there are letters falling from the sky! Only they're all mixed up.

"This might be the new ending we need," PB says thoughtfully.

ARRANGE THE LETTER PIECES TO WRITE A NEW ENDING TO THE STORY.

CE AN YD
AN LL NI DA
DT GH T HE

an d t

If you think the ending is "And they danced all night,"
TURN TO PAGE 69

If you think the ending is, "And they did all right,"
TURN TO PAGE 116

If you think the ending is "And the day became night,"
TURN TO PAGE 53

POTIONS
AND JUNK

"Let's go left," LSP says, and they hurry through the tunnel on the left, leaving the monster behind them.

The tunnel leads to a big wooden door. Finn pushes, and it creaks open. Inside, there are tons of shelves filled with jars and jars of mysterious liquids and powders.

"Potions and junk," Finn says. "I wonder if they're all magical."

"Well, Astrid is a witch, so probably," Jake says. "Maybe this book will tell us."

There's a big book on a fancy stand. Jake opens it to a random page. Only it's not so random. It's a lucky flip.

Jake whistles. "Check this out," he says. "There's a jar in here that holds part of Astrid's soul. It's her 'Sweet Soul.'"

"Let me see that!" LSP says, pushing Jake aside. She reads out loud what Astrid has written. "'I found a way to remove the part of me that makes me nice. It was such a nuisance. Now I can do my own thing without remorse.' Ha!"

"I get it," Finn says. "If we find the Sweet Soul and put it back in Astrid, she'll be nice again and stop capturing people and getting her monster to eat them and stuff."

Jake points. "There's a map that shows where the soul is."

"Then let's hurry up and get it already!" demands LSP.

HELP THE GANG FIND ASTRID'S SWEET SOUL

Follow the clues to find the jar that contains Astrid's Sweet Soul. Trace your path with a pencil. Be careful—if you choose the wrong jar, you may end up with a dangerous surprise!

1 Start at 1A. Move one square to the right.

2 Move five squares down.

3 Move five squares to the right.

4 Go down three squares.

5 Move six squares to the left.

6 Go up three squares.

7 Move four squares to the right.

8 Go down three squares.

9 Move one square to the right.

10 Go up two squares. You've found it!

Lumpy Space Princess Saves the World

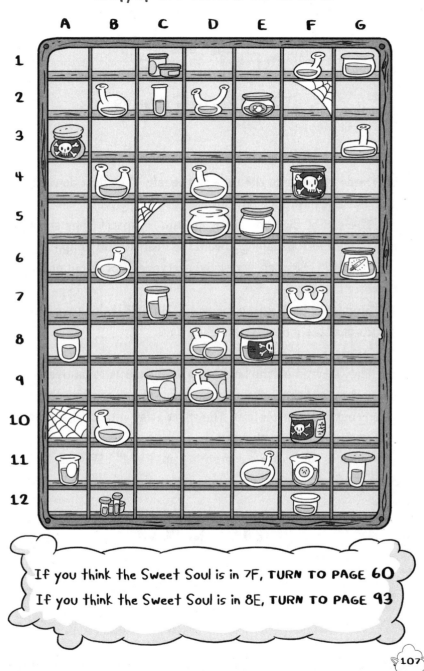

If you think the Sweet Soul is in 7F, **TURN TO PAGE 60**

If you think the Sweet Soul is in 8E, **TURN TO PAGE 93**

OUT THE WRONG END?

LSP leads everyone to the tube on the left. They float down it, and Jake and Finn slide down it like it's a playground ride.

The end of the tube opens up into . . . space! They shoot into space and start falling toward the nearest land lump.

"I did it!" LSP cries. "I rescued everyone! I got us out of the monster's mouth."

Finn looks back at the monster. "Uh, LSP, I think we just came out of the monster's butt," he says.

"Gross, Finn!" LSP says.

They all land on the land lump. LSP expects to be treated like a hero, but the Lumpy Space People are all grumpy about sliding out of a monster butt. They float away without thanking LSP or cheering or anything.

"Thanks for messing everything up, Finn!" LSP yells, and then she floats off.

THE END

WRONG WAY, DUDE!

LSP floats down the tube, and Finn and Jake jump in after her. It's all fleshy and bumpy in there, and then suddenly, they fall.

"Gross!" LSP yells. "What the lump happened?"

They're inside some kind of tunnel, and it's filled with sticky wax. Jake tries to stretch out of the wax, but it's on him like glue, and he can't move. Finn gives a massive groan and tries to break free, but he can't. And LSP can't even move her lumps.

"I think this is earwax, dude," Jake says.

"Well, we're stuck in it," Finn says. "What should we do?"

"I don't know," Jake says. "This was your adventure."

"Get me out of here!" LSP wails.

"Not gonna happen," Jake says. He looks at Finn. "Hey, this adventure feels a lot shorter than usual, doesn't it?"

"Definitely, man," Finn agrees. "Definitely. Guess we should have taken that other tube instead."

THE END

THAT's NO BLACK HOLE!

LSP jumps into her parents' car. "We totally need to save them! Hurry up, you guys!"

Finn and Jake jump into the car with LSP. She speeds off the land lump and flies up toward the black hole. It's closing, so it doesn't suck them in.

As they get closer, they notice something. The black hole is part of an enormous, black, blobby thing. Then two giant yellow eyes open up over the black hole. Yes, eyes!

"Oh my glob! It's a monster!" LSP yells.

"Finally, I get to punch something!" Jake says, stretching out a rubbery arm.

But before Jake can punch anything, an orange streak whizzes past the car.

"What the lump was that?" LSP asks.

TURN TO PAGE 99

CARL'S
DINNER

LSP transforms her lumps into the shape of a . . . beard?

"What the math?" Finn says.

"I don't know what I'm doing! I can't hurt my best friend!" LSP cries.

"That's not your best friend, that's a nasty Space Witch," says Jake.

Astrid transforms back into her witch self. "Aha! I win! And you lose. Albedo Odebla!"

She points at them, and those laser lassos come out of her fingers again. She corrals LSP, Brad, Finn, and Jake, and then takes off on her rocket broom. She rides right up to the mouth of the big monster.

"Eat up, Carl!" she yells, and then she hurls them inside.

"This is lumping unfair!" LSP yells as the monster gobbles them up.

THE END

TOAD
PRINCESSES

"You call this clean?" Maja shrieks when she returns to the cauldron room. "You made it even worse!"

"Come on, Maja," PB says. "We can work something out."

"Just lumping let us out of here!" LSP shouts.

Maja's eyes flash with anger. "That's it! I'm out of patience."

She points at LSP and PB, and electricity flies out of her fingers.

Zap!

LSP is now a purple, lumpy toad. PB is a pink toad.

"This is so lame—*croak*!" says LSP.

THE END

I'M SO LUMPING HAPPY!

LSP sighs. "All right, Astrid. You can take the part of my heart that loves Brad. Because I love my parents. And because Brad is going out with Melissa, anyway."

The witch grins. "Perfect! Now hold still!"

She points a finger at LSP. "Parallax Xallarap!" she yells.

LSP feels a rumbling deep inside her lumps. It doesn't hurt, but it's weird. Then some purple light streams out of her body, and Astrid catches it in a bottle.

"Thanks!" she says. "You can't do that spell without the consent of the victim—I mean, volunteer."

LSP fights back tears. "You got what you wanted. Now keep your end of the deal."

"Fine," says Astrid. "Supernova Avonrepus!"

Things get all swirly and crazy and stuff. LSP's head feels all mixed up. One second, she's still in Astrid's prison. The next second, she's back in Lumpy Space. Finn and Jake and Brad are there—and her parents—and all the other Lumpy Space People are back on their land lumps. The monster is gone.

"What happened?" Finn asks.

"I made a deal with the Space Witch while you were, like, all frozen," LSP explains.

"Nice going, LSP," Jake says.

Brad walks up to her. "Thanks for getting me out of there. I was wondering—do you want to get back together?"

"Oh, Brad, yes!" she cries. She has never felt so happy. Then she remembers. "Wait a second. This doesn't make sense. That witch took the part of my heart that loves you, Brad. But I still love you with every lump on my body!"

"Guess she shoulda taken your lumps, too," Jake says.

"But she didn't!" LSP says. "Stupid witch."

"So you'll be my girlfriend again?" Brad asks.

"Yes!" says LSP. "Come on, Brad. First, you've got to break up with Melissa. Then we need to get some chili cheese fries!"

★ ★ You earn 99 ADVENTURE MINUTES. ★ ★

THE END

FREE?
NOT EXACTLY!

"It's princesses!"

"You're wrong," says Cuber. "The theme connecting the stories was the five vowels—*A, E, I, O,* and *U.*"

"Does that mean we're stuck here forever?" Lumpy Space Princess asks.

"No, silly," says Cuber. "I'm not a gibbing meanie. You're free to leave! Have fun guessing next time!"

Suddenly, LSP and PB are not in the book anymore. They're back in the library. But things are way different. The whole library is filled with magical purple mist from the wizard's ball. It's so thick, it makes them cough.

But even worse—books are flying around and falling off the shelves. LSP and PB get sucked into another book.

"At this rate, I calculate it will be three thousand five hundred and sixty-seven years before we get out of this library," PB yells.

"That is sooooo lame!" LSP yells back.

THE END

TOO LATE!

" 'And they did all right,' " Princess Bubblegum says out loud.

Nothing happens at first. Then the words all blow away on the wind, and PB and LSP are still stuck in the book.

"This is lame," LSP says. "I'll never get out of here and never save my parents!"

"We can follow the wind and get those letters," PB says. "Come on."

LSP and PB follow the wind and pick up the letters. Then they put them together to make the right ending: *And they danced all night.* It works! They get out of the book, find the book on black holes, and go back to Lumpy Space.

When they get there, it's eerily quiet. There's no sign of any Lumpy Space People. No black hole. No Finn and Jake.

"This is terrible!" LSP wails. "Everyone's gone!"

PB puts a hand on LSP. "Don't worry. We'll find them somehow."

LSP hopes her friend is right. Otherwise, she'll be the last Lumpy Space Person in the whole world!

THE END

YAY,
FREEDOM!

"Nadir Ridan," Miguel says, and the cages of the beasts all open! The room is suddenly filled with creeping, crawling, flying, growling, hopping creatures. It looks kind of dangerous, except the beasts are all super happy to be free.

"Everybody follow me!" Miguel shouts.

There's a stampede as all the beasts leave the room they've been held captive in for so long. LSP, Finn, and Jake follow them out. But when they get into the hall, Astrid is there, and she looks angry.

"What is this?" she shrieks.

Zap! A cat-headed spider hits her with a sticky web.

Glop! A slime creature blasts her with gross goo.

That witch isn't going to stop them now. They all creep, crawl, fly, growl, and hop past her as Miguel leads them to a way out.

They pass the prison cells, and there's Brad again—the real Brad. LSP remembers the witch's spell.

"Nebula Aluben!" she cries, and the real Brad is freed.

"Thanks," he says.

"Whatever," says LSP. "Let's get the lump out of here!"

Miguel leads them to a room filled with rocket brooms. There's a big, clear window leading to a flight deck, and LSP can see the enormous monster still hanging out outside.

"Hey, Miguel! What about my parents?" LSP asks. "That lumping monster swallowed them."

"Oh, you mean Carl," Miguel says. "No biggie. I got this."

Miguel grabs a rocket broom and flies out to Carl. He talks to him for a second. As he flies back, Carl starts coughing up the Lumpy Space People. They fall onto the land lumps below.

"Thanks," LSP says. "That was pretty decent of you."

"You're welcome," says Miguel. "Hey, I'd hate to fly off and never see you again. Want to go on a date?"

LSP looks at Miguel, who looks like Brad. She looks at real Brad. One of them just rescued her parents. The other one is dating her best friend.

"Sure, Miguel!" she says, loud enough for Brad to hear. She checks out the expression on real Brad's face. He looks crushed. Awesome!

"Let's go get some chili cheese fries, Miguel," LSP says, hopping on the broom behind him.

Then they fly off into the starry sky.

★ ✹ You earn 89 ADVENTURE MINUTES. ★ ✹

THE END

BEEP . . . BEEP . . . BEEP

Clik gives Finn the transponder, and then tells them how to get to the monster's stomach, which is where all the Lumpy Space People are.

"What are we waiting for, then? Come on!" LSP insists.

They shoot down some tubes, and then they fly through a flap at the end of a tube. They're in the stomach! Jake grabs onto the side and grabs Finn before they can both fall into the steaming pit of stomach acid below. The Lumpy Space People can float above it, so they're all safe.

LSP's parents come floating up to them. "Finn! Jake! We're trapped in here! That flap only opens one way!"

Finn and Jake climb back to the flap and try to pry it open, but it's weirdly sealed shut.

"Too bad you don't still have your sword," Jake says. "You could pry it open."

"But I have this," Finn says, holding up the transponder. It's a little black box with a red button. "Wonder what it does."

He presses the button. Then the transponder starts to send out a sonic signal.

Beep . . . beep . . . beep.

"Hey, maybe somebody out there will hear the signal and find us," Finn says hopefully.

"What a lame machine! I thought you were a hero, Finn, not a loser," says LSP.

"He is not a loser, young lady. He's trying to help!" scolds Lumpy Space Queen.

And then all the Lumpy Space People start whining and arguing and yelling. Jake looks at Finn.

"I hope somebody hears that signal soon!"

THE END

WHAT's YOUR ADVENTURE TIME?

Mathematical!

It's time to add up all those Adventure Minutes you earned, and figure out your super-ultra-awesome **Adventure Time.**

So, how did you do? Did you save LSP's parents? Did you find Brad? Did you explore the books in the library and get out in time to save the day?

Write your total super top
Adventure Time here!

Want to get an even bigger **Adventure Time?** Flip back to page 1 and start the adventure anew, making different choices!

ANSWERS

PG 9

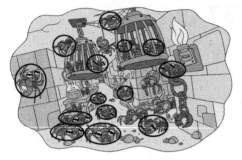

PGs 11-12

PG 17

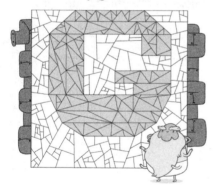

PG 27

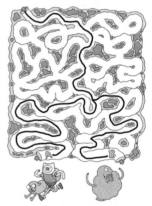

PG 30

AD MI TT WO GU es TS

PG 32

M	G	I	O	R	B	I	T
O	E	S	U	N	V	G	E
O	I	T	T	T	T	A	S
N	S	T	E	N	A	L	P
N	R	O	M	O	A	A	A
O	A	S	O	T	R	X	C
V	T	R	C	I	D	Y	E
A	S	T	E	R	O	I	D

GIVE IT TO ASTRID

PG 35

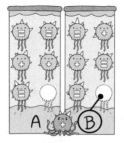

PG 38

RATPY DOG
P A R T Y G O D
CLEAMNIRE
M A R C E L I N E
LILBY
B I L L Y

LSP should turn into a
B R E A D

PG 44

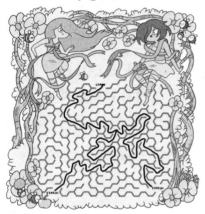

PG 47
TRANSPORTER

PG 51

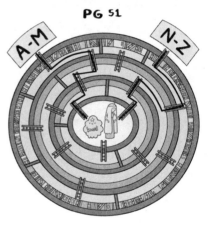

A-M   N-Z

PG 58
44 CELLS

PG 68

PG 65
NADIRRIDAN

PG 75
RIGHT

PG 78

PG 85

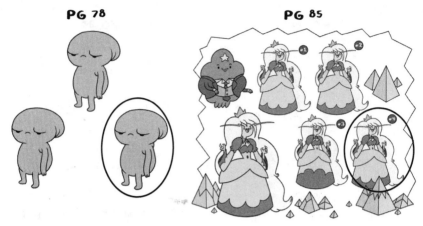

PG 98

PG 101
NEBULA
ALUBEN

PG 107

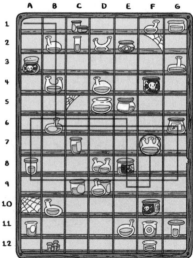

PG 104

AN DT HE YD AN CE
DA LL NI GH T

**AND THEY
DANCED ALL
NIGHT**